THE MAN FROM KASHMIR

THE MAN FROM KASHMIR

A Novella

Muddasir Ramzan

BLOOMSBURY
NEW DELHI • LONDON • OXFORD • NEW YORK • SYDNEY

BLOOMSBURY INDIA
Bloomsbury Publishing India Pvt. Ltd
Second Floor, LSC Building No. 4, DDA Complex, Pocket C – 6 & 7,
Vasant Kunj, New Delhi, 110070

BLOOMSBURY, BLOOMSBURY INDIA and the Diana logo
are trademarks of Bloomsbury Publishing Plc

ISBN: HB: 978-93-69528-05-9; eBook: 978-93-69525-58-4

2 4 6 8 10 9 7 5 3 1

Typeset in Fournier MT by Manipal Technologies Limited

Printed and bound in India by Thomson Press India Private Limited

MIX
Paper | Supporting responsible forestry
FSC® C010615

To find out more about our authors and books visit www.bloomsbury.com
and sign up for our newsletters

For the people of Kashmir
in whose survivance
I found my roots

‘History . . . is a nightmare from which I am trying to awake.’

James Joyce, *Ulysses*

Prologue

The mountains above Poshmarg stood like white-shrouded judges, leaning over the town to witness a night that refused to be still.

The air was a frozen whetstone, sharpening the silence until it bled.

Amid the sound of bullets and the heavy thud of shells, the people rushed towards the Jamia Masjid, a masterpiece of deodar wood and grey stone, seeking the safety of the collective and the sanctuary of the sacred. Its minaret, carved with the geometric memories of centuries, had absorbed the prayers of generations.

The people emerged like ghosts; they moved in a frantic silence.

Suddenly, the stillness of the night was broken by a sound that defied the serenity of the architecture.

A woman's screams erupted from the heart of the prayer hall. The microphones caught the frequency of her cries. Each scream tore through the veil of the night.

Prologue

It was the sound of a soul being pulled through a needle's eye. Every few minutes, the silence would reclaim the air, only to be shattered again.

Each scream was a hook, pulling something hidden from the depths of the town's collective soul.

It was the sound of a struggle against the inevitable, a violent negotiation with the dark.

It lasted a moment. The town held its breath until its lungs burned. It lasted a lifetime.

A wail so pure it felt as though the wooden minaret might splinter into dust.

Then, the world became quiet. For a heartbeat, Poshmarg was a tomb.

A thin, sharp trill sliced through the mosque's speakers, breaking through the frozen dark.

It was the first breath of a child…

1

The Unnamed

. . . what happened in their absence hit them like death. Poshmarg wasn't their home any more.

Cradled between the two mountains, the houses lit up by gleaming electric bulbs made Poshmarg look like an ill-formed constellation. With no trace of the moon, the night was darker than usual. It was the last day of 1990, and many residents of the town were watching a special New Year's Eve telecast at Masterji's house, which had the town's only colour TV. Masterji had gained notoriety for having bought it while returning from Haj. The more religious elders accused him of bringing Satan's doll to Poshmarg, the cause of growing immorality among the youth. Even so, Masterji considered the TV one of his prized possessions.

That night a big explosion hit the uniformed men's camp at the entrance of Poshmarg.

The blast was followed by countless gunshots, and the rattle could be heard across Poshmarg.

Farooq, who had already left Masterji's house with some friends, rushed home to join his family. They stayed indoors, worried mainly about Ayesha, Farooq's sister. She was due to give birth at any time.

Meanwhile, the loudspeaker blared. Everyone held their breath. 'Let's gather at the mosque. It's better to stay together,' announced Jalal-ud-Din, a respected muezzin.

Farooq immediately began to put some essentials and a few blankets in a bag. He asked his family to hurry, saying, 'It is not safe to stay at home.'

But his father, Ahmed sahib, locally known as Bubb, decided against leaving the house.

'Why don't you understand the gravity of this situation,' Bubb said. 'It isn't safe to go outside. And Gul has also not come back yet. What will he say if he comes back and sees that his wife is gone?'

Gul, Ayesha's husband, was living with them at this time, as Ayesha had returned to her mother's house for the birth. They were not living with his parents for they had disowned him for marrying Ayesha. The couple lived in their own small home, far away, on the outskirts of the town.

'It's not safe to stay here either,' Farooq said, upset. 'It would be easier to deal with the danger together in the mosque.'

Mouj, his mother, interfered. 'But how will you reach the mosque when bullets are still being fired in the air? Trust me, the uniformed men won't come here.'

'A home without an elder's counsel is a house without a roof,' she added after a pause.

'Mouji, they'll be here soon. We will manage. This is not the time to wait.'

Realising he would not be able to convince them, Farooq left the house with Ayesha.

The biting cold and Ayesha's pregnancy slowed their pace. There was no movement on the road. A naked chinar tree cast a protective shadow over the area that opened a small path to the mosque. In the darkness, the exchange of gunshots on the upper side of town was visible, as if someone were throwing kangris filled with hot embers.

They somehow managed to reach the mosque. Most of the town's inhabitants, to Farooq's surprise, were already there. The mosque's green walls reflected the light of the soft golden bulbs, mixing the shadows of the people appearing on the wall like sketches, some very big and some tiny – depending on their movement. Filled with anxious women, nervous men, restless children and weeping babies, the mosque was Poshmarg, and Poshmarg was the mosque. As they moved further into the crowd, they saw Gul, and Ayesha ran to him in relief.

'They stopped me on the road,' he said and looked at Farooq. 'Thank you for bringing her. I was so worried.'

Many people were telling each other what they were doing when they had heard the blast. The elders of the town were trying to calm the people. They arranged kangris and quilts for them to help them endure the cold night and asked them to respect the sacredness of the mosque.

The youth were still in high spirits. One of them joked about Masterji's presence in the mosque, to which another said, 'Yes, I am seeing him in the masjid for the first time after he returned from Haj.'

An elderly man, who heard what they were saying about Masterji, told them off angrily, saying, 'This is not the time for jokes.' But the group of youngsters continued giggling behind their hands, and one of them dared to mention that if they don't laugh, how would they live. 'Asav ne, te lasav kith paeth,' he said.

The sound of another blast made all of them silent.

No one dared to talk, not even the children. They prayed to God to save them.

In this deafening silence, Ayesha felt restless. She had not anticipated going into labour at that moment, but she felt uneasy. A half-empty shelf of religious books, primarily copies of the Quran, was anchored to the wall on the left side of the prayer hall. Ayesha went and sat beneath it. She felt sweat on her right hand as she touched her forehead; it was as if a gust of hot wind had hit her whole body.

She realised the time had come – she was going to give birth. She covered her mouth with her hand, but she was in griping pain. Soon, the women noticed and rushed to Ayesha's aid. Someone summoned Rahat Maas, the midwife who was sitting in the opposite corner. By then she was unable to stay silent with the pain.

While the women were busy, the men covered that side of the mosque, making a partition with whatever was available. Everyone was worried – about the impending danger and for Ayesha.

Gul got hold of a small carpet and pushed it under Ayesha with the help of Farooq and the midwife. Gul's presence made Ayesha feel a little comfortable. It was quite difficult for Farooq to witness the screams and struggles of his sister, but when Gul put his arm around Farooq's shoulder, he regained courage. He always thought of him as his elder brother and a mentor.

After a battle that seemed to stretch into eternity for Ayesha, as she writhed, her son tumbled out into this world. As soon as the newborn was cut loose from the umbilical cord, he found himself in the arms of his father. Farooq was overjoyed upon seeing the baby. He got hold of the local imam, who looked anxious. He had worn his prayer cap upside down and had forgotten to remove his shoes before entering the mosque. Following the tradition practised in Poshmarg, the imam took the baby in his arms, kissed his forehead, and said the azaan in the newborn's ears.

Meanwhile, grim-faced uniformed men carrying weapons, who had lost many of their companions in heavy shelling, reached Poshmarg seeking the assailants.

In all this, Jalal-ud-Din was horrified when he realised that he had forgotten to switch off the loudspeaker. Nobody else had thought of it either, maybe because the microphone was next to the mihrab while they were sitting away from it. Ayesha and the baby's cries had been pouring through the town and, as if a bugle call, they had summoned the uniformed men.

The angry uniformed men cordoned off the mosque. Furious, they were looking for the insurgents: 'Where are they? Where did you hide them?'

It seemed the insurgents had escaped the very moment they had hurled heavy shells at the camp.

The long night began anew.

Almost every man, young or old, received a beating. The room next to the mosque's entrance, which was used for ablutions, was turned into an interrogation chamber. Gul was spared because Ayesha had begged the uniformed men to let him stay beside her and tend to their baby.

The residents caught in this violence craved the light of day. It was the darkest and the longest night in the history of Poshmarg. When the soldiers left, they took with them the young men, including Farooq, to the camp as suspects for further interrogation.

Already fragile from facing the torture of the uniformed men, the remaining people in the mosque were shattered when they looked outside and saw that dawn had already broken.

The time of morning prayers was long gone. The elders of Poshmarg murmured to themselves that God would forgive them because He watches everything.

Ayesha and Gul were sitting frozen in their corner when a voice rang out, saying, 'Ayesha!'

It was Bubb and Mouj. The sounds from the mosque had carried through the town, and later someone had gone running through the dawn to tell them that Ayesha had given birth to a boy. The two had abandoned their fears of leaving home when it was confirmed that their daughter had given birth in the mosque.

'Oh God bless, Ayesha is fine, the baby is fine, shukur Robas kun,' Bubb said in relief. Her eyes shimmering with tears of joy, Mouj reached out to gather Ayesha into her arms. 'Farooq was right. What would we have done if you had stayed at home – you would have had no midwife. It was God's will after all. Khudayan kor sahal! Where is Farooq? He was right to bring you here.'

Their happiness disappeared all too soon when they were informed that Farooq was taken by the uniformed men. Mouj strongly suggested that a group of senior men visit the camp, talk to the head there, and free those young men who were taken away. Bubb and the residents present there agreed, and a group of them headed towards the camp.

Meanwhile, at the mosque, people gathered around Ayesha to congratulate her and see the baby, their smiles and laughter briefly masking their fearful pale faces.

Most people felt sorry for the situation in which she had had to give birth to her son; others just stared at them with pitying eyes before they gathered their nerves and returned to their houses. Gul and Mouj waited for everyone to go. Gul took away the bloodied blankets as Ayesha and Mouj sat on the floor with the baby.

The air that morning was heavy with despair.

The news of uniformed men breaking Masterji's TV spread across Poshmarg. Masterji lamented the loss of his prized possession, the fragments of which lay mixed with the shards of glass along with a toppled chair, a broken vase of flowers strewn over the floor with the water seeping into the carpet. There were mixed reactions to the breaking of the TV: the elders, while disapproving the method, were happy to know that Satan's doll was finally annihilated. The youngsters felt terrible about losing their only source of entertainment, and for Masterji.

Something had changed.

All the young adults who were taken away to the camp for further interrogation were released by the next morning.

When they came back, they carried with them a rumour: the uniformed men would not stop inspecting Poshmarg until they had hunted down all the militants. With the rumour going from one house to the next, as each worried mother hurried across the street to tell her neighbour, the terror from the night before began to creep back into the day. The people in the town didn't want to be tortured again. Many decided to leave the town to escape the wrath of the uniformed men. One by one, they made preparations to leave by night.

If there had been no trouble, Ayesha's family would have arranged a big feast to welcome the newborn; there would have been wazwan served to everyone.

Even people in the neighbouring towns had heard the bombing and gunfire and were afraid. As the town's residents slowly began their drift to other towns, so too did the story of their long night – and the news of Ayesha's son's birth. Meanwhile, scores of people from neighbouring towns put their fear aside and came to visit Bubb's home, each one with a gift and a request –

they leave Poshmarg and come to stay with them. Poshmarg was no longer safe.

Bubb turned his mind to the preparations for the seventh day. Tradition demanded the aqiqah and the naming ceremony be held, regardless of the chaos outside. For Bubb, honouring this ritual was the only way to restore a sense of order to their shattered world. They spent the day preparing, sending invitations to the imam and the midwife.

Gul personally requested the imam to look for a good name for his son – something unique – which would suit him well. The streets were brittle with a silence that threatened to break, but Bubb and Gul couldn't wait for peace; the aqiqah could not be delayed. They tracked down the only taxi owner in town. For the aqiqah, besides sheep they also needed to get izband, fresh kulchas, and enough chicken, lamb, and fish to honour the imam and the warin, the midwife.

In the evening, when Mouj went to share food with their next-door neighbour she found the house locked. The neighbour had spent the long night at the mosque; walking home hand in hand with Mouj, she had insisted that nothing would make her leave her house.

Mouj moved about to check on the other acquaintances and found only a few old men and women in Poshmarg. Terrified, she rushed home. Gul consoled her, assuming what they had heard were only rumours, and they had nothing to be afraid of because they had done nothing wrong. Besides, how could they leave? Their guests would show up tomorrow. Mouj tried to convince Gul and was frustrated that Gul would not believe the truth that was right in front of her eyes. But made uncertain by Gul's belief and his joy, she soon gave up.

Mouj cooked fish with hakh and some tomatoes in an earthen pot and a special lamb soup for Ayesha. Slowly, the family's forgotten happiness was revived over their shared dinner. The weather changed abruptly, heralding snow. Tired after their sleepless night, they locked the house's main door and went to bed earlier than usual.

Thinking of the deserted town and the rumours, Bubb shifted restlessly in his bed on the first floor of the house that overlooked the street. He leaned on a cushion, his kangri held in between his thighs by his left hand, and adjusted the quilt over his legs. In the dead of night, he heard some noises. He fluffed up the quilt, let go of the kangri, and went straight to the front window.

Hiding himself carefully behind the curtains, he saw a group of men carrying guns in the light being reflected off the snow.

The silence made an almighty crack with the first kick in the door. They moved to the windows, rattling at the panes with their hands, and then to the other sides of the house. When they came back to the door, they started over. Bubb's heartbeat was loud in his chest, and he walked silently to wake Farooq who was still sleeping on the bed. Together they moved carefully to the ground floor, where they found Mouj trembling in the lobby. Bubb made his way with quiet, deliberate steps to Ayesha's room in the back of the house. He found her shaking in fear, with Gul holding the baby who remained asleep.

Bubb's eyes met Gul's, confirming an unspoken agreement – they would not open the door. They stayed still, silently waiting. It worked; maybe the gunmen believed that the house was empty, they assumed.

After a while, the noise of the gunmen's banging reduced and eventually ceased. The entire family sat in Ayesha's room as the faint light of day slowly trickled in. As morning unfolded, Gul accompanied Bubb outside to see if the house had been damaged. The white snow wiped out the edge of their fear; the soldiers would not come back soon.

'We must leave now. It's not safe to stay here. What if they had broken the glass, unlocked the door, and found us. We could have been beaten. Killed,' Farooq said, while Mouj set before him a cup of nun chai as she moved mechanically through her morning routine.

'Yes,' Gul said. 'I'm sorry, Mouji. You were right.'

'Allah was merciful,' said Bubb, staring at Farooq. 'Have tea first. We'll think about it later. It will be difficult to travel in the snow.'

As they drank their chai, they did not realise that the uniformed men had returned. They had forgotten to lock the outer gate after coming inside.

They had come in large numbers, in big bulletproof vehicles and jeeps rigged with chains on wheels to avoid slipping on the snow. They stopped at the big chinar tree and jumped out of them and followed those who were already in the town. Silently, the swarm of uniformed men cordoned off Bubb's house in minutes. They had been informed that the assailants who had bombed their camp were staying in that house. They were prepared for an armed encounter.

As the family sipped their tea, they crashed into the kitchen wearing long white snow boots, their guns raised. In a minute, they had kicked the samovar, and the tea spilled all over the place as the baby began to scream. Ayesha, holding the baby, moved to Mouj in fresh terror.

The uniformed men pointed their guns at Farooq and Gul, shouting over each other and over their pleas.

'Where are they,' they yelled, shaking Farooq by the collar. 'We know they are your friends, you coward! You left the town to go learn to weave carpets? Do you think we are stupid?'

The anger reflected in their eyes and their loud voices, the sound of which overpowered Farooq's pleas. One made a call for the rest to beat them, but they didn't move. Maybe it was the sight of crying women. They wanted to know where the insurgents were. They were sure that they had found the men who had attacked them.

Using Gul and Farooq as shields, they searched every room and corner of the house. They went through the cupboards of everyone, scattered and tore apart heaps of possessions – also Ayesha's clothes, coverlets, and baskets of kulchas, fresh fruits, and dried fruit.

After their search failed to reveal any rebels in the house, they accused the family of having a secret hideout. Dragging Farooq and Gul to the storeroom, they gave them spades and made them break the inner brick wall. When they found nothing, they grabbed Gul and Farooq and dragged them to the jeep, hitting them along the way. The doors of the jeep shut behind Gul and Farooq as they were made to enter it while the women spilled out of the house.

Ayesha shouted and tried to run after the jeep to the camp, but Bubb stopped her. He brought her back home. Her body was still recovering from childbirth.

They wondered if they had made a mistake by not opening the door to them at night. But the uniformed men hadn't said a word about making an attack at night. Perhaps it had not been them.

'Maybe the ones in the night were the ones who attacked the camp,' Mouj said.

'The militants?' Bubb raised his voice. 'But there were so many of them. And why would they come here?'

He was afraid. He understood the danger. His decision to keep his family home felt like a trap. He'd seen the crowds leaving and believed they misunderstood the risk, but his choice to keep his family at home felt less like protection and more like a danger. He could not understand why the militants would come to his home.

'Some informer might have seen those rebels coming to our house last night,' Ayesha said. 'If it wasn't the uniformed men, who else could it have been? Maybe they came for food.'

'There's no time to think about that now. We need to visit the camp first; we need to get Gul and Farooq,' Mouj said.

Bubb tried to put some courage back into them.

'Everything will be all right. Khudayas mangiv himmath! Stop crying and clean the house. We'll get them back. Be brave and stay indoors.'

Going door to door, Bubb gathered a few other elders present in the town and went to the camp for a second time in the week.

The major allowed them to see him in his room, made them sit, and asked them to share their knowledge of the militants they had seen in Poshmarg. But they hadn't seen any, an old man answered, bewildered. Bubb sincerely spoke up about the incident of the previous night. The major told Bubb and others to be vigilant about the militants; their plan was to destroy Poshmarg, he warned. He told them to inform him if they saw any movement of the terrorists.

A shudder went down Bubb's spine when he saw Gul and Farooq, who looked physically broken and emotionally destroyed. They were made to sign in a fat notebook, which had their names neatly scribbled, before being released from the camp.

With Farooq and Gul held up on both sides by the elders who had accompanied Bubb, the quiet party limped back home. Tears rolled down Ayesha's cheeks as they were lowered into their beds, unable to sit up.

They had to postpone the name-giving ceremony. 'We saved their lives,' said Mouj. 'We can do this later.'

As soon as the two men recovered from their injuries, Farooq, Gul, and Ayesha packed up their things and left their home with the unnamed baby. They begged Bubb and Mouj to come with them, but the two elders refused, and responded typically, relying on the sayings of the old to defend them. 'Wande tsalih, sheen gali, beyi yi bahaar,' they said, referring to the arrival of spring when the winter passes.

'Someone has to be in the house,' Mouj said. 'Who will let you in? Besides, we are old. We are not a threat.' It was true; and the journey would be arduous too, with uncertainty about where they would go. Once again, Bubb and Mouj stayed behind.

It took five long weeks for a tentative calm to settle over Poshmarg, finally signalling that it was safe to return. During the first fortnight, Gul and Farooq had occasionally risked daytime trips back to Poshmarg to check on Bubb and Mouj, otherwise they were mostly relying on whispered news from their hosts. However, Ayesha, restless and uneasy in the homes of distant relatives, had kept them moving. They spent the final two weeks far from the reach of the town, clinging to the hope that Bubb and Mouj were safe and well.

While they waited for their return, Ayesha, Gul and Farooq called the unnamed baby Jigra or Gasha and sometimes simply Myon Gobur. He was, after all, their heartbeat, their light, their dear child. But the people they stayed with, seeing the child was born into such chaos, sometimes teasingly called him Jangpoot, a war-child.

Gul, Farooq, and Ayesha were desperate to see Bubb and Mouj. They had waited long enough. On their way home, the three decided they would visit the imam the next evening to finally officially name their unnamed son and get the approval from the elders in the family.

When they arrived home, Ayesha rapped at the door with her knuckles. 'Mouji!' she called out, happy. 'We've come back! Let us in!'

There was no response.

They waited and tried again. Farooq joined in, shouting for his mother. When there was no response, Gul broke a window glass and let himself in, shouting for both Mouj and Bubb through the house. They found the house ransacked yet again, the same pantry wall broken down, and the print of muddy jackboots all over the floor.

Making his way to Bubb's room, Farooq walked through the door and paused. Gul and Ayesha entered behind him and were stopped in their tracks: Bubb and Mouj were lying frozen on the floor, eyes still open. They had died holding each other's hand.

After the burial of Bubb and Mouj, the silence was shattered by a sorrowful resurrection.

'Ahmed,' Ayesha said under her breath.

'I want to call him Ahmed – after my dear Bubb.'

2

Awakening

'Why,' he whispered to the silence of his own mind, 'would it only be the Muslims who resent this incursion into our home?'

Dawn had only just crept across the sky when Ram opened his eyes. It was the day of the cricket match, and the adrenaline made it impossible to go back to sleep, even as his limbs felt heavy with early-morning laziness. He counted down the minutes until he finally swung himself out of bed. The air felt different today – no school, only the promise of a historic clash between India and West Indies.

His uncle, Upendra Dhar, peered through the door and smiled at the boy's restlessness. 'Not ready yet?' he teased. 'I thought you would be out already. Get dressed; I'll drop you.'

Ram wore his favourite jacket and jeans, and rushed through breakfast. He pulled on the boots he had meticulously polished the night before. As he stepped out of the house, his uncle was already waiting in the car with their driver, Lala. Upendra looked at him with a mix of pride and mischief. 'See, here's our Ram, our hero. You should join Bollywood.' Ram gave him an exasperated look, though a smirk played on his lips as they set off.

In the car, Upendra's urge to make fun of Ram did not abate. 'Ram has some message for me,' he told the driver. 'His aunty has whispered something special in his ears.'

Ram rolled his eyes, but a smile took the sting out of his pretended impatience. 'Uncle, it is what she always says – loads of instructions to be careful, and so on.'

His tone suddenly turned serious. 'Listen – no jokes today, all right? She's right. I know you don't get into fights but don't mess with the city boys. Just take it easy. And if you can't find a bus or a taxi, you know where to come, don't you?'

'Yes, your office. Why won't I find a bus or a taxi?'

He grimaced. 'You never know. Times are strange. But never mind that. Right. You must enjoy yourself. Here's some money, take it.'

'No no, Uncle, I don't need it. I have enough,' Ram protested. He felt embarrassed.

'Oho, my young saint, never turn down a gift. Besides, who are you calling Uncle? Will you deny your father the chance to spoil you?'

He pushed the money into the pocket of Ram's shirt, and he accepted, uncertain still but resigned.

The bearded driver's eyes flickered to Upendra's reflection in the mirror, and he could sense the sudden awkwardness that had crept into the car. 'Arre sahib,' he said, 'it is a blessing to have a child who refuses money instead of asking for it! You don't know my daughters – they would have taken those notes and then had their hands in my pockets to check for more before I could even say anything!'

As Upendra eased into a belly laugh, a smile came upon Lala's face – he was happy when his boss was happy.

'Dapyomas boznavtam chus ba banday…' As Upendra and Lala broke into a song together, the tense atmosphere in the car finally dissolved. Ram leaned his head against the glass, watching the poplars flicker past like skeletal sentries lining the road.

Winter had come earlier that year, and that morning the air was crisp and cold, hitting Ram's face through the window that he had stubbornly kept open. The old men selling boxes of apples and corn, fixed at regular intervals along the road, were already in their pherans, though it should have been another month before they were brought out.

They drove past Lalchowk, peaceful in the morning stillness. The shops were still closed. They stopped the car right at the entrance of the stadium.

'Remember,' Upendra warned one last time, 'you have to be careful. You have money with you in case you need it. And you come back straightaway, if there is any trouble.' Ram gave his yesses absently, wanting to hurry out of the car, shouted his goodbyes as he ran towards the crowd at the stadium door.

People had come in droves and were waiting for the security personnels to let them in. Ram waited, like all the others, in excitement. Soon there was an announcement, and he saw people making queues and jumped ahead. In a few minutes, the line was so long that it stretched up to Burn Hall School, like a snake making turns and curves. Scanning the gathering, Ram's eyes landed on Ishfaq. His childhood friend was perched right at the barrier with his companion, Bita. He was happy to see Ram there.

Finally, after the security guards at the gate had frisked him and checked his backpack, his ticket, and his identity card, Ram was allowed inside.

Ram, Ishfaq, and Bita took their seats right in the front row. All around them, fans were trying to clamber over the barriers, desperate to reach the dressing rooms for a closer look at the teams. Some hoped to shake hands and some dreamed of autographs from their favourite cricketers, but the area was heavily guarded.

India chose to bat first. As soon as the match began, people started booing and jeering at the Indian cricketers. Ram looked around, bemused. This was not expected; he wondered whether this was the trouble his uncle had warned him about. Ishfaq was laughing gleefully and began shouting with the rest. 'Come on then, you useless whoresons!' he said. 'Do you even know what to do with a bat!'

Ram's mouth dropped, delighted and appalled in equal measure. Ishfaq had been a teacher's pet at school, and he had never heard him speak like this. Bita looked at him, looked at the team for a moment with uncertainty, then decided to join in. 'If you don't know how to handle a ball, go back and ask your mother!'

Ishfaq whooped with joy and grabbed Bita around the shoulder, jumping excitedly and joining in the inarticulate jeering. Ram looked at them and thought of how he had always prided himself on acting like a grown-up. He had draped his griefs around his shoulders like a heavy cape, never allowing the feckless glee of being young and foolish to reach his heart. 'Not today,' he thought.

'Yeah!' he shouted, throwing his voice into the heaving beast of the crowd's baying. 'You'll get a no-ball if you've got no balls!' Not great, but he was a beginner; Ishfaq and Bita both cheered and started hooting.

As the chant swept through the stands, Ram surrendered to it. With his friends' arms slung around his shoulders and the crowd echoing his own words back at him, he felt a sudden, violent surge of joy. They settled down to watch once the game began in earnest; but during the breaks, some people went on to the main pitch. A single barrier had come down, and the crowd funnelled through.

Though the pitch hadn't been fully wrecked and they could have continued the game, the disturbances created by the local people who tried to dig the pitch made them call more security on the ground. The presence of heavy security there heightened the crowd's frenzy and fury; it could do nothing to stop the insults from flowing. The mood of the match had suddenly grown darker; what had started as mischief and banter was turning into serious, angry jeering. Ram looked at Ishfaq, and he stared at the gathering crowd with an unwavering gaze; it was no longer a joke – it mattered now, in some inexplicable way, that they made their loyalties known while the world was watching. This was their chance to show, once and for all, exactly who they stood behind, and who they refused to support.

Ram grew quiet, uneasy; he did not have any quips to make any more. 'Send the fuckers back to where they came from!' an unknown voice shouted, followed by roars of approval. He silently took this as cue – this was trouble, and he knew what he had to do.

He left the stadium and went straight to his uncle's office, stopping briefly to pick up something to eat from the sweet shops on Residency Road. When he reached his uncle's office, carrying some extra for his uncle, his uncle was happy to see him. It was the first time Ram had been there so early in the day. Upendra took him around the office, introducing him as his son to his colleagues and associates, who were discussing the match. They had heard about what had happened during the game. Upendra told them that Ram had come from the stadium, and they wanted him to narrate exactly what had happened.

Ram related in as much detail as he could recall what had taken place, taking care to avoid any mention of the jokes he had made. They had heard more – it had started getting dirtier during the second innings. The people made it difficult for the Indian fielders to play, particularly those near the boundary of the field. India lost the match, and with it the dignity with which they had first entered the field.

Upendra and his associates were worried about this behaviour of some of the Kashmiris, and what it meant for the future. They were not meant to be mindful of their religious identities. They were not Hindus, Muslims, Sikhs, Christians, or Buddhists; they were only Kashmiris. They were talking about the impact the whole fiasco could have on the Valley. 'But this incident, and the resentment among the Muslims can change the face of the Valley,' one said.

Watching the old men argue, Ram felt a cold realisation settle over him. None of them suspected that he had been part of that very crowd, shouting alongside them. The distinction they drew felt like a fracture he couldn't ignore. If the Valley was his home, then the anger belonged to him too.

3
The Widening Gyre

While relishing a brisk evening walk in Poshmarg, Gul and Ram stopped at a clearing along the path, nestled between rice fields that lay dormant after harvesting.

Children, who had created a makeshift cricket pitch, were rushing towards a pile of clothes, mostly pherans, which they had taken off and collected to serve as wickets. Some put them on, and some ran off clutching them in their hands. The scene reminded Gul of the days they too used to play cricket in their neighbourhood. All the family would join in; the elders and their neighbours would also participate.

'Those were the golden years. Why did we grow up?' Gul sighed.

'It was the best,' Ram responded. His mind too had wandered into his childhood. 'The more you know, the more you grow. The more you grow, the more quickly you begin to lose it. The taste of happiness.'

'That's right,' Gul said, lingering over the words. 'The taste of happiness.'

They continued walking, engrossed in their conversation, oblivious to their surroundings.

'Have you ever thought about what you will do?' Gul asked.

'About what?' Ram asked.

'Getting a job?'

'It's not easy to get a government job, Gul. It's not at all easy. I had no idea it would be so difficult.'

'Yes but, Ram, don't you want to start the next stage? Of life? We will be able to just as soon as we get a job.'

'What? Do you mean getting married? Having children and working ourselves into the ground to provide for our family?' Ram laughed, a little bitterly.

'Maybe after years of hard work we might save enough money to build our own house – miles away from our parents and brothers. Great! And then we die. Our lives are mapped out for us whether we like it or not.'

Gul looked at him sideways. 'Girls won't give you a second look if you don't have a job.'

'What girls?' Ram asked.

Gul laughed. 'You want to get married and not be alone. But you can't do that without a job.'

'Haha! Maybe. Everyone is after money and good family status here. This money shit! Earning just to barely live.'

'But everyone has to earn money,' Gul said.

'Whoever invented this concept of money should be hanged. Hanged until all life escapes them. Who was it, do you know? Can you imagine! We could be living freely now, if it wasn't for him.' Ram's sense of humour had returned, and Gul was relieved to see his anger recede.

'Yes, what a fool he was. But we are all fools now.' Gul laughed. 'Would you say Lalita loves you because of your money?'

'You know I have no money.'

'Exactly. Not everything has to be about money. Come, let's go home now.'

'I mean it,' Ram said. 'There has to be a world beyond making money. To dream. To live.'

Gul was quiet, but uneasy.

He put on his cap. 'How are you not cold?' he asked. 'You can put your hands in the pockets of your trousers.'

'Okay, but I'm not thinking about the cold,' Ram said.

Gul went on, insisting, 'How can you not feel it. See, maybe nobody is here today because of the cold. Those children run around so much and stay warm.'

'Maybe you're right,' Ram said, looking around distracted. 'Yes. Those trees were not bare when we came here on Friday – I remember seeing the leaves.' He looked around. 'It's getting late.'

'Yes,' Gul said. 'I know. That's why we're going home.'

Ram looked back at him and smiled. 'What are you doing tomorrow?' he asked. He wanted to talk more about a world without money. He realised how gently Gul had been taking him out of his black mood and was filled with a rush of affection for his friend.

'Nothing,' Gul said. 'Didn't you see? There's a strike.'

Ram looked away as they kept walking.

'No,' he finally said, fed up. 'I didn't see. These days you don't have to see anything, nothing matters. One day the world is at peace, the next day it's filled with blood.'

'God,' Gul exclaimed miserably. 'I wish we could do something.'

They walked in silence.

'You know where to go,' Ram joked. 'Join the revolution if you're serious.'

Gul baulked. 'No, I don't know where to go. You tell me where I should go. How many revolutionaries have you been speaking to?'

'Stop talking rubbish. You said you wanted to do something.'

'And that's all there is to do? That's your big idea? Join freedom fighters? Is that our liberation?'

'Don't if you don't want to,' Ram said. 'It's not like the uniformed men have tortured us. Why bother.'

Gul looked at him, a small smile on his face, not reaching his eyes.

'Don't take it like that,' Ram said, rolling his eyes. 'You know what I mean. We're good living our lives like this. What are our wealthy elders doing? Sitting on their money quietly! Do they ever care? How is it our responsibility to fight injustice when we are poor? Don't you see it's all they give you if you are poor – the dream of azadi?'

Ram's face was hot. Gul looked at him and decided to say it.

'You are a Hindu, Ram,' he said gently. 'You don't have to worry about azadi.'

Ram kept walking, now a little faster. 'Don't be so stupid,' he said. 'Sometimes I wish my family had also migrated. I would have loved it.'

Gul mischievously elbowed him in his side.

'Go on, then? You have relatives in India; you can move anytime. Leave me behind, all alone here.'

Ram suddenly stopped and stood still.

'What is it?' Gul asked, his playfulness vanishing.

'Do you hear something?'

Both silently looked around but heard nothing, only the whispers of the twilight.

'It's nothing,' Gul said finally. 'Come now. You fear too much. Put on some music.'

Ram put a song on his phone and began to sing out loud. He stopped the music right at the line about childhood tantrums, 'Lakchaaruk machar myoun', and caught Gul's hand, bringing them both to a sudden halt.

'Why did you put it off?'

'Gul, there's someone behind us. Don't panic.'

Turning around, they noticed the gun first, and then the uniforms. Their voices unexpectedly tore through the silence as they began shouting at them to stop. In the dim light, they froze, their eyes desperately searching for any other civilian who could help them or at least be their witness. They were alone. In less than a minute, they were surrounded by the men who were shouting furiously at them, as if they had caught a couple of rebels. Slowly, they raised their hands.

Suddenly the serene road, their favourite route to walk, became surreal. 'We are civilians, sir,' Gul muttered, while glancing at Ram to gather his courage.

The uniforms did not listen, instead turning them around and away from each other. The frisking began. 'Saaley, stand straight. Identity cards. Now.'

Ram swiftly pulled out his wallet from his pocket and flapped it open, showing his card to the cop, who grabbed it out of his hand. Gul fumbled while searching his pockets. 'Shit! Sirji, I forgot – I don't have my wallet and my card.'

Ram looked up and saw Gul being made to march away and dragged his eyes back to the uniformed man whose hands were on him now, pulling him in the opposite direction. He was taken to a poplar tree, all the while his hands up and a gun pointing at him, where he was frisked again. The hand holding the gun did not waver.

Gul was brought over to where a uniformed man was sitting on a large stone, behind some apple trees. In the darkness, the two friends lost sight of each other.

'I'm just a student,' he said, dread making his words trip over his tongue. 'I live here – in that town over there. It is fifteen minutes away. Ask anyone who lives there. I left my house in a hurry and forgot my identity card. We were just taking a walk.'

Other uniformed men gradually faded away.

'Lagta hai tujhe seeda karna padega,' the uniformed man said. 'Are you working for the militants?'

'Sir, please, I am telling you I am a student…'

Half an hour later, Ram and Gul were brought back to the same spot. They could hear the sound of each other's heartbeat merge into one, a loud thumping echoing fear. 'Don't come this way again,' a uniformed man said coldly. After a pause, he added, 'Go straight home. It's not safe here.'

When Ram asked meekly for his card, they laughed at him and told him to come and get it tomorrow from the camp.

Quietly, they made their way home, half-turning their heads to look behind every few steps.

The road seemed longer than they remembered it to be, while they stumbled over the bushes and small trees in their path. As they half walked, half ran, Ram tripped over a branch and fell hard.

'Shit,' Gul said, stopping and picking him up. 'Are you all right?' As he picked him up, their breathlessness filled the night air. The interruption forced them to take a breath.

'They could have killed us in this lonely place,' Ram said in a low voice, his fury upon Gul without warning, without direction. 'I told you to always carry your identity card. They would have let us go straightaway if you'd had it!'

'What are you saying?' Gul tried not to shout. 'Stop thinking like a child. If it was like that, they wouldn't have kept you for so long.'

'He asked me why I was with you,' Ram said. 'A Muslim boy. You of all people should know that you need to have your ID with you.'

'They do this to everyone. You belong to their religion and they still questioned you.'

Ram's breath evened out as they both resumed walking, the sudden anger evaporating.

'I told him you were like my brother,' he said to Gul, offering half apology, half defence.

Gul let out a huff of laughter. 'Do you know what he asked me? If I was here to meet girls! I didn't say anything and then he said, "Where do I find a girl here?" The one in the hat then tried to provoke me, "How can you marry your own sisters?" I told him we don't, and he shot back, "Cousins are sisters too, you behenchod."'

Ram looked at him and started to laugh.

'Well,' he said in between breaths. 'At least now we can say we've been tortured by the uniformed men.'

Gul looked at him and started to laugh too.

'We're going mad,' he said. 'Let's just go home.'

They tried to erase the fear from their faces as they prepared to meet their families.

As they neared Ram's house, Gul greeted his uncle who had emerged from the main door. Ram's family considered Gul to be far more sensible, brighter, and more promising than their own son, and they were glad the two were friends. Ram's uncle affectionately hugged Gul, asking if he wanted to stay for dinner.

'No Uncle,' he said smiling. 'My mother is waiting.'

As he crossed the street and entered his own house, Gul's mother came out as she did every day and asked the question she always did.

'Where were you?' she asked, her arms crossed over her chest. 'You're late.'

As he always did, Gul looked away, and said, 'With friends.'

'Some men with long beards came looking for you,' said his mother.

'Who were they?'

'I don't know. They were in a hurry, they said they wanted to speak to you only.'

'Maybe they're from the mosque.'

As they sat down for dinner, Gul's father began. 'Son,' he said. 'You know that if you want to make anything of yourself—'

'Not today, Baba,' Gul said, interrupting him. 'Please.' His parents watched with concern as he got up from the dastarkhawn without eating and went up to his room and closed the door.

The next morning, Gul woke up early. It was a quiet morning; the strike meant that the streets were empty, and there was no sound of traffic to cut through the song of birds.

Lying in bed, he slowly grew restless. He got up and walked over to the window. He stared with unseeing eyes, until his mind became aware of the scene outside.

It was snowing.

He spun around and ran out of his room. 'At least put on your shoes!' he heard his mother shout as he rushed out of the door.

He stood outside, face tilted up, experiencing a sense of joy he had not felt in a long time.

Flakes of snow whirled effortlessly before his eyes and settled as a thin, soft layer on roofs, the tops of trees, and every surface they could find. It was the season's first snowfall, which had arrived earlier than expected.

After lunch, his father asked him to help in freeing the branches and trunks of trees from the snow. Soon Ram joined them too. After finishing the task, their hands shivering with cold, they came indoors, and Gul's mother served some tea and brought them kangris.

'Is everything okay? You're quiet,' asked Gul when they were finally alone to talk. 'Is it about last night?'

Ram flopped on to his bed. 'I wish! No. It's Lalita again.'

'Don't worry; she'll call you when she's calmed down.'

'I just didn't want to talk last night. Wanted to sleep. She wouldn't stop calling, and when I finally picked up, we had a fight.'

'Ram, Lalita truly loves you. I've seen her affection for you in her eyes. The way she looks at you, it is special. She will not leave you,' Gul said.

Though Gul, wary of the handcuff of relationships, hadn't indulged in any romances;

he knew too well how words, if not used correctly, turned into venom, allowing misunderstandings to always rule relationships.

Whenever he tried to search for understanding, people seemed to be clamouring to find offence.

From the window, Gul could still hear the children playing excitedly in the snow outside, making snowmen and hurling snowballs at each other. The thought of their carefree playtime held him spellbound.

He turned to Ram. 'Let's go out again. Wait for a second while I grab my camera. I want to take photos of the kids playing in the snow.'

Ram stood up. 'I'll go get my jacket.'

4
Unknown Gunmen

. . . *Ayesha is determined to not let the fire of revenge consume her son.*

When it felt like summer in the daylight and winter in the night, and the air was languid, an unknown gunman shot Ram dead.

Soon after the bullets were fired, the clouds began to weigh heavily and finally came undone as sheets of rain, as if the sky itself were weeping. Out in the open, just outside his house, Ram's body lay on the grass, waiting for the rain to wash the blood away.

A young boy heard the gunshots and, unmindful of the danger, ran over to see who it was. When a group of frightened people, about six in number, saw him running towards the spot from a distance, they felt encouraged to assist and followed him. Confused, the boy looked at Ram's body on the grass; unsure if he was dead or merely injured. He didn't dare touch him. He waited for the people he saw coming towards him, squinting his eyes in the rain. When they arrived, one of them went closer to the body and gently turned it over. They recognised Ram.

He had been shot thrice, once in his head and twice in his chest. The spots where the bullets had entered Ram's body had darkened. The blood was still oozing out. The rain fell in bold strikes, mixing with his blood to release a strange, sharp aroma – like almonds scorched over a flame. It soaked into the ground; the soles of everyone's shoes turned muddy and red.

When the people carried the dead body to the courtyard of Ram's house, they found Lalita unconscious, lying on the floor of the veranda. However, she had not fainted because she knew it was her husband who was shot; Lalita was afflicted with such fits whenever anything unexpected happened. This time, it had been at the sound of the second gunshot.

Their two-room house was coated in a thin layer of clay, with its makeshift roof atrophying, the rusty metal structure leaning on to the porch. The house and its shabby courtyard that day looked drearier than usual, perhaps also mourning its owner's demise.

When Lalita opened her eyes, she suspected she had woken up into a bad dream. She felt empty. The world in which she had been happy seemed far away, unreachable; but how could this happen in mere minutes, she thought. The freshness of the nostalgia made her believe it was not real.

She took a deep breath and asked herself, 'How could they kill Ram? What wrong had he done?'

She couldn't make sense of it. She wanted nothing but to look back into the world she had just lost. She felt stuck in this world without her husband.

Ram's family had not even come.

It was a chance for them – his revered Karkun family, his older brothers and uncles – to cease their anger. He was already dead to them for he had run away from home to marry Lalita, a girl from a Goar family they despised. Perhaps they were sorry about his death. However, they continued to act like he had never existed, like he was not their own blood. Perhaps if Ram's parents or his favourite uncle, Upendra, were alive, it would have been different, Lalita thought. Perhaps this would not be the world in which he was dead.

With her emotions bleeding into each other – desolation, doubt, outrage, shock – Lalita tore at her velvet green pheran.

She begged her family and everyone else to leave her alone soon after Ram was cremated. Relatives and others had to, in keeping with custom, visit regularly and those close to the family had to stay with them to grieve for twelve days. Both to help the bereaved and to help the deceased move on into the afterlife.

Like other customs, Lalita had defied this one too.

Lalita herself buried her husband's remains under the peach tree that stood on the right side of the courtyard. He would be where he would be remembered. She fought with everyone, particularly her uncles and other elders in Poshmarg, who wanted to scatter the remains of Ram in the Gangabal and let him join the dead. They watched with pursed mouths as she knelt on the ground, digging a hole for his ashes. It was a practice reserved only for the holiest of priests. Almost everyone left her house upset; they felt disowned and disrespected.

Only her mother and Ayesha remained.

Ayesha, Lalita's childhood friend, stayed with her to ease her pain. She understood why she was angry with her relatives and family friends.

They had always gossiped about her remarriage and now whispered among themselves that perhaps Ram had been involved in a crime.

Some suspected that he had earned money as an agent of the state, an informer. Otherwise, why would he be killed in broad daylight, right outside his home?

Her father's family lived on the other side of town, but she had not visited them after she had married Ramakrishna. Ram and Lalita had decided to elope after realising that a union of their two families was impossible. They were secretly married in one of the Arya Samaj temples. Together, they had abandoned their traditional life for the peace they found in each other.

But all that had changed. Lalita's mother had only come now, after Ram had died. It was the first time Lalita had seen her since the last night she had spent at her own house before eloping to make a home with Ram. It had been Lalita's brothers and uncles, realising Ram's family would remain absent, who took care of all the funeral arrangements; from helping to cremate Ram and performing all the pujas to arranging food and shelter for the visitors. Now that Ram was dead, they were willing to forget the shame Lalita had brought to them. But when they tried to take Lalita with them, she wouldn't leave her own house – her dream home with Ram. The smallest reminder of Ram – a stray comb, his scent, his tea mug, his clothes – would cause Lalita to burst into tears. She struggled to grasp the finality of his death, but the reality refused to take hold. Her mother, intimately familiar with the hollow ache of widowhood, refused to let Lalita suffer in isolation. When Lalita insisted on remaining in the house she had shared with Ram rather than returning to her family, her mother moved in, providing a silent, steady presence.

Fifteen days after his murder, a man came to Lalita's house early morning and asked for a glass of water. Even though he was unfamiliar, Lalita invited him to breakfast. He was surprised at her offer but quickly collected himself to politely refuse. She went into the kitchen to get him a glass of water. Strangely, by the time she came back with the water, he had left. She spotted a folded page near the main door where the stranger had been standing a moment before. Something in Urdu was written on it. She wanted to read it, but she couldn't make sense of it.

In the quiet weeks before his murder, Ram was the lamp, coaxing Lalita through the dark forest of illiteracy – a journey through English, Hindi, and Urdu. She returned each evening from the community school, a fresh start for those without formal education, to be met by his persistent encouragement. Yet, for all their effort, she had so far only learned to write her name and address. Curious about what the letter said, she quickly made tea and some rotis, served it to her mother, and told her that she would be back soon so she shouldn't worry.

'Change your clothes,' her mother called out when she saw Lalita leaving. 'Wear that maroon pheran. That suits you very well. Don't go like this.'

'It's okay,' Lalita responded and closed the outer gate.

Holding the letter tightly, she walked across town to see Ayesha and Gul, the only ones she trusted. They all were happy to see her and the couple welcomed her warmly into their newly built house.

Ram and Gul had been best friends since childhood, but with time they had stopped seeing each other as often as they used to when they were growing up. But that had never stopped their friendship. Ever since Ram's death, Gul and Ayesha had been taking turns to regularly visit Lalita.

Lalita kept looking at the bare walls and the kitchen pots stacked at their temporary spots along the walls. Lalita knew the house had not been ready for them to move in. The openings where there should have been windows were covered with thick polythene sheets for the time being, though it was not safe, neither very helpful in keeping the cold at bay.

'Shouldn't you have at least gotten windows by now?' she asked Gul. Ayesha glanced at her and smiled.

Gul and Ayesha had saved money to buy this portion of land where they had built a house. Gul looked at her kindly and responded, 'I have to be honest when I contact the carpenter. I can't lie and say I will pay him soon, then make him work, and disappoint him when he is done. I am saving money for the windows; give me some time.'

Lalita and Ayesha both had relatives who had built new houses at the same time. They pointed out how smart they were – they lived in their decorated homes and still owed money to the constructors and workers.

'I cannot be like them,' said Gul.

While they were chatting about the difficulties of earning a livelihood and building a new house, Lalita took out the letter and gave it to Gul, who read it aloud.

'If you want to know who killed your husband and why, come to see us at the entrance gate of

Government School tonight, 9.30 p.m. Your well-wishers.'

What followed was a strange moment of silence. Lalita let the information sink in. There was no clue in the letter about who could have written it. There had been rumours about Ram, that's all she knew. That he was killed by some rebel group.

'Maybe it wasn't true then,' she said out loud, 'that the rebels killed him.'

Ayesha nodded. Gul paused, thought again, and turned to Lalita.

'Yes. You remember the other killings from last month – those groups had publicly announced why they had killed them.'

Gul took out the letter again and turned it over. There was no evidence to suggest it was written by a rebel group.

'It could be from a person and not a militant outfit,' he said. 'Did you recognise the man who brought you the letter?'

Lalita's face dropped, and she shook her head.

She may have lived all her life in Poshmarg, but she didn't know many of its residents, and she couldn't always remember the names of those she did know.

At the sight of the letter, the heavy tension in Lalita's face finally began to lift. For a moment, she felt like she was in the right world again.

She had always thought that Ram would have never done anything dangerous, but the manner of his death made her wonder that maybe he had betrayed her. Now she would finally know whether her husband had been the man she knew, or one that had committed some crime.

Ayesha said it would be dangerous to go alone to the meeting point and Gul offered to accompany her. As Lalita stood up, they protested. They wanted her to stay for the day or at least for lunch, but she was worried about her mother. Ayesha walked her to the makeshift outer gate of the lawn, put her right arm over Lalita's shoulder and drew her close. 'Everything will be all right,' she said.

A faint smile was on Lalita's face as she left. Ayesha's eyes followed her as she walked towards her home. Lalita was not even thirty, but she walked, her steps heavy and slow, like tired old women. As she reached the top of their road, Ayesha watched as she collapsed in the middle of the street. Shocked into movement, Ayesha called for Gul, and they ran to her with Ahmed following them. Ayesha was the first to reach her. She took hold of Lalita's arms. Lalita lay unconscious with her hands inside the pheran. More people gathered, while Gul and one of his neighbours held Lalita in their arms and brought her back into Gul's house. They sprinkled some water on her face. She regained consciousness and was again herself.

She had been having these fits for some time and was taking medication for it, she told them. She tried to stand, still wanting to leave, but was scolded by Ayesha for even thinking about it.

Ayesha packed some food and called Ahmed to deliver it to Lalita's mother. Ahmed hopped on his bicycle and left, and upon his return he reported that she was happy that Lalita was taking some time off. 'Tell your mother to force Lalita to stay with her for some days and not worry for your Zoon Ded. I'll be fine.'

Ahmed had been given instructions to not mention Lalita's health to Zoon Ded, and if possible, to bring her with him and lock up their house. Zoon Ded assured Ahmed that she was fine. Besides, Lalita's brother would be visiting her soon, she claimed.

After Ahmed came back they all sat down for lunch, a little later than usual. Because it was Sunday, Ayesha had cooked red beans with meat and lotus roots and rice for lunch – Gul's favourite. He often said that the smell of cooked local rice made his stomach dance. They preferred local rice, not the foreign variety, which the people had started to get at cut rates in Poshmarg.

After lunch, they let Lalita get some rest. She kept trying to sleep, and when she couldn't, she walked out to the veranda to join Ayesha. She made Lalita sit down and began to comb her hair, setting it in order. Soon, they were lost in a discussion about how their lives had changed. As the sun moved into evening, their conversation moved backwards in time, from their present to their childhood, which they referred to as the silly age.

Lalita recalled the day she had told Ayesha about Ram and their plan of eloping. That day had had a remarkable effect on their friendship – Ayesha had promised her she would be there for Lalita all her life. They laughed at how they had planned to get their children married: 'If you have a boy and I a girl, or vice versa, we will marry them and secure our friendship for posterity.'

Lalita's laughter turned into a solemn smile, and she grew quiet. Sensing the heavy stillness that clung to her and to disperse the gloom, Ayesha mentioned how that day they couldn't collect enough dry leaves in the orchards and had felt embarrassed for coming home with their half-loads.

'Those were beautiful orchards. The whole area is empty now,' Lalita said.

'Yes,' Ayesha said. 'It's the railways.'

'They've ruined the beautiful hills.'

'We were blessed with apple orchards.'

A heavy silence hung in the air. 'We could have done it if my daughter had lived,' Lalita's words pierced it.

The child had survived for only a few hours. But that had been some time ago. Grief that had kept its distance had found her again. Gul arrived, quietly bringing nun chai for the two friends, a small comfort in the heavy silence.

As the evening approached, Lalita's urge to leave rose again. But Ayesha and Gul did not have to struggle to make her stay, for Zoon Ded had come to their rescue. Wearing a brown embroidered pheran, a blue shawl covering her white headscarf, she entered through the outer gate of the house. 'Ayesha! Gul! Lalita!' she called their names.

'Ded!' Gul cried when he saw her come into the door, a pleasant surprise. Zoon Ded was adored by everyone for her wisdom and kindness, though she had not supported Lalita when she had married outside the caste.

Gul and Ayesha felt a special softness towards her, because she had cared for and looked after them when Bubb and Mouj were killed. Her arrival made the day more special for them.

Ded looked at her daughter, recognising the signs of a fresh breakdown, and spoke with a voice softened by understanding. 'Dayi kari sorie theek,' she whispered, her words a gentle prayer for her daughter's peace. Gul told her about the letter. But as soon as Zoon Ded heard about the idea of her daughter going to meet unknown, potentially dangerous men, she was terrified. She announced her displeasure at her resolve for going through with it.

They had dinner. Lalita wasn't hungry. They thought she was anxious about meeting the unknown person. As they sat down together to eat in the kitchen, she fell on to the floor, again unconscious. They picked her up and made her lie in another room. When she woke up, she seemed confused and frustrated, and immediately tried to stand, but found her knees buckling under her. Ayesha pleaded with her to not move and to sleep. She needed to see a doctor, this was not normal, even for her. But Lalita was adamant she would not. She didn't want to lose the chance of knowing her husband's secret.

Her body was covered in sweat. No doctor would be available at night. A medical assistant lived on the other side of town. At ten, even she had to concede that it would be impossible – they decided Gul would meet the unknown person alone and, if possible, bring some medicine for Lalita.

'Ram was taking me to a special doctor. I already have some medicine at home. Don't worry about me. I'll visit that doctor tomorrow,' Lalita promised, trying to stand up, still wanting to go with Gul. But everyone else was firm. She was not to go anywhere.

At this point, Zoon Ded spoke up.

'I don't feel good about this, Gul,' she said. 'You are putting your life at risk. Ram is dead. I think you should not go there.' Lalita looked at her with betrayal.

Gul glanced at her and then back at Zoon Ded. 'Don't be afraid. I have seen worse. He was my childhood friend. I have to know the truth about him. Don't you? We all deserve to know who killed him and why,' he said.

'Then tell my sons. They should go with you. Don't go alone.'

'Why disturb them now? It's too late. I will be fine. Don't worry about me. I have your prayers.'

Before he came out of the house, he wanted to talk to Ayesha. She was very nervous about the idea of Gul meeting unknown men; but she couldn't say so out loud. She looked down, not meeting his eyes; she didn't want to let him feel her fear. Gul eyed her with affection as he saw her cleaning the kitchen, refusing to look at him, and finally left. Ayesha sighed; her eyes filled with tears when she saw Gul leaving. She gazed at him as he walked through the lobby to the main door, and when he opened the door to leave the house, she came inside the kitchen immediately. A strange emotion overwhelmed her – less worry, more regret.

Ahmed ran out after his father.

Gul turned to face him and knelt down, holding him as he spoke, 'Look, Ahmed, be careful. You are seven years old already. You are the man of the house when I am away. Lock the outer door and be careful.' The boy nodded. Gul stood up and left.

The night was darker than usual. A curse of darkness followed these two families. The darkness was no obstruction for Gul. He could have walked the path to the school with his eyes closed; his feet knew every stone and turn from years of routinely crossing this path.

He encountered several elders hurrying towards home after securing the mosque's gate, for the time of the final evening prayer had long slipped into night. They asked if everything was all right and why was he out so late; Gul told them he was fine, that he had to meet someone. They prayed for his good health and left him.

On reaching the school, Gul looked around cautiously but couldn't see anyone. He slowly entered the school garden through the half-open broken gate, but he couldn't find anyone there either. He reached the main building and leaned against the wall to wait. Even though he felt like smoking, he didn't dare light a cigarette.

Gul felt a little cold in his shalwar kameez and thought he should have worn a sweater over it. There was a big walnut tree on the backside of the school. Maybe, he thought, that was where he would find him. He decided to check and walked back out through the same half-open broken gate.

As he stepped out, the darkness yielded two figures. One, muffled up in a long pheran, moved with an unnatural stiffness, as if the garment were a borrowed skin. The second simply obscured his face with a mask. He paused, the question hanging heavy in the tenebrous air: were these the faces he had come to meet? Gul greeted them anyway; they remained silent. In that moment, he knew they were the ones who had written to Lalita.

'Lalita sent me here,' Gul said directly. 'She could not come. She is ill.'

But the air returned only a hollow echo. The silence, immense and unbroken, stretched into a long, suspended moment.

The two strangers turned away and spoke to each other under their breath, while Gul listened carefully.

'Who else is with you?' finally the one wearing a mask broke the silence.

'I am alone,' Gul replied immediately.

'We want nothing to do with you. Tell Lalita that she has lost her only chance.'

'Tell me if it is you who killed Ram.' He found it difficult to understand their accent.

'Me? Are you mad?' The voice was getting increasingly angry.

'Then who? What did he do? Tell me.' Gul's voice rang out with a steady, unshakable confidence. He focused, sifting their words. Their accent was clearly not local, but a bewildering confluence of Hindi and Urdu that defied Gul's attempts to place its origin.

'Listen, we wanted to meet Lalita, to make her understand that Ram wasn't good for her. She should live with her parents now. They will find someone else for her,' said the second person.

'But who killed Ram, and why?'

'It's none of your business, Master. Now go.' The voice came from behind the fabric of the pheran, spoken by the man who seemed clearly ill at ease in his disguise.

'So you know me?' Gul asked. He felt a strange peace come upon him. 'I can see you're holding a gun inside your pheran. I won't say your name. I swear I won't say your name. Trust me, I won't say your name.'

'Why would I tell you that? Why would you ask? Don't make me angry.'

'Please,' Gul said. 'I want to know what Ram's crime was and who killed him.'

'Master…' The voice paused and spoke again. 'Ram wanted to help Lalita. We felt for Ram – I did! – when he mentioned Lalita's tumour. I wasn't the one to fire the gun.'

Gul took a minute. 'Lalita has cancer...' he said, his voice shaking. 'Who are you working with?'

'Why are you asking!' the other man said loudly.

'Master, we can be anyone,' said the man wearing the pheran. 'What did the newspapers say? "Unknown gunmen." Leave it there.'

'But—' As Gul started to speak, the voice filtered through the mask, no longer angry. He spoke quietly. 'His mind is keen; he'll place us quickly. He knows the truth about Ram and letting him walk away is no longer an option. We can't afford this risk – he is a threat that must be silenced now.'

The two men looked at each other. The one wearing a mask pointed a pistol at Gul. The other one, who knew Gul was a teacher, sat down. He put his head between his legs and covered it with his arms, all the while staring at Gul's feet.

Gul was paralysed with fear. His throat felt dry. 'Please,' he said.

He tried to clear his windpipe and opened his mouth again.

'Please. I have a family. I won't tell anyone. I just wanted – Lalita had asked me to find out. I swear. Please.'

The masked man looked at him silently.

'Please,' Gul said again.

He shot three times. Once in his head, twice in his chest. The figure of Ayesha in her wedding dress was the last thing Gul saw before his body hit the ground.

The first man crawled over to Gul's body, held him and wept. He threw away his gun, slapped and cursed himself like a madman for his helplessness. When he stood up, he turned and slapped Gul's killer, who held him as he struggled and whispered something in his ear. The first man calmed down. He turned and looked at Gul's dead face again, moving closer to shut his eyes, and then dragged him to the school's broken gate.

His companion collected his gun, and they disappeared in the darkness of the night.

5
The Carpet Weaver

A tapestry of silicon silk, with a map of United Kashmir richly embroidered on it. The hues shift dramatically, starting from the deep, bloodshot reds of Kashmir, transforming into lush emeralds and radiant sapphires.

By the time Farooq reached his adolescence, he had started dreaming of becoming the first medical practitioner in Poshmarg. As a late teen, he could not go to medical school. But Bubb had used his contacts to apprentice him to the esteemed Dr Jan, allowing him to work and study within the walls of the city's most reputable clinic.

Farooq had got high marks in science, which he had studied for his senior years at school, and was a quick learner. If he had continued working at the doctor's clinic, he could have earned a medical licence, not to be a doctor but to open a medical store in Poshmarg.

But things changed unexpectedly. It was not the first time he had missed a workday at the doctor's clinic. It had happened a couple of times. But the last time was when Fatima finally came to see him at the clinic one morning, only to inform him that her family was looking for a groom for her. He left work at once, again, and went to his sister's house.

Confused about how to break the news about Fatima to his family, he asked her to do so. She liked Fatima, Ayesha said. It was just that she belonged to Syeds, and Syeds preferred to marry among Syeds only – though not always. But she wanted to help him. She could see in his eyes that Fatima was important to him. It was no childhood infatuation.

Ayesha set off for her parents' home, troubled. She wanted to tell her husband, but first, she had to see her parents.

It was evening. Bubb and Mouj were relaxing on the veranda, joking about how the chirping of groups of mynas on a tree in their lawn seemed like they were fighting about which group owned the tree. In the dim light, Ayesha appeared, offering a cheerful 'Assalam-o-Alaikum'. Bubb gathered himself while responding warmly to her daughter, and Ayesha sat beside him, facing Mouj.

'Is everything all right?' asked Mouj. Her daughter did not often make the journey across town from her new house without any warning.

'Yes, all is well,' Ayesha said.

'And Gul is fine?' Bubb enquired.

'Fine, dear Bubb,' she said.

'Good. Good,' he said cautiously.

Mouj stood up, moving towards the kitchen, when Ayesha grabbed the bottom of her pheran and pulled her back to sit down. 'I just had tea,' she said. 'I have come to talk about Farooq.'

'What happened to him now?' Bubb asked with a half-smile.

'He is worried about you. He was saying someone needs to be with you, while he is working at the clinic. He doesn't want you to be on your own.'

'Really. If that is so, why didn't you and Gul live with us when we wanted you to? But you were so adamant about living by yourselves in that shack you call a house.'

Mouj enquired gently about her well-being, noting that she had prepared a meal specifically tailored to nourish both Ayesha and the life she was carrying.

'Dear Bubb, we have had many discussions about it. You know very well that Gul wants to have his own land. He wants our child to have a house of their own. We'll come here when the date is close. Besides, there is something else.'

'And what is that?' Mouj asked.

Ayesha was silent for a moment. Hesitant, trying to find the proper words to say it.

'We cannot read minds,' Bubb said. 'Out with it!'

'Farooq's marriage,' Ayesha blurted out.

'What! Why? He's not even twenty-two!' Bubb exclaimed. 'He has only been working at that clinic for some time, hasn't finished even a year. How can he get married now?'

'Actually there is a girl I had in mind. But she has started getting offers from many families. Before her parents fix her marriage, I want you to talk to them about Farooq.'

Bubb was quiet. Then he enquired, 'A girl you had in mind? Not Farooq?'

'Never mind that,' Mouj said, looking quickly at him. 'Who is she? Who is her family?'

'A girl who lives down the road,' Ayesha said.

'Here in Poshmarg?'

'Yes.'

'But … that is the Syed mohalla,' Mouj said, still confused.

'Exactly.'

Bubb's face fell. 'Are you talking about Shafi sahib's daughter? Fatima?'

'You knew?!' Ayesha said incredulously.

Bubb looked away and putting his hands on his knees started to stand up. 'You're getting late,' he said. 'It's time to go.'

'Bubb! What's the harm in trying?' Ayesha looked to meet Mouj's eyes. But the darkness of the evening covered the space between them.

Bubb walked towards the kitchen, refusing to say anything more. Mouj stood with her and then walked her to the door. She didn't say a word; her gaze was fixed on nothing in particular, as if she were searching for answers within herself.

Gul had been waiting for her, and she could finally tell him everything – her brother was in love with a Syed girl, who came all the way to his workplace to tell him she was going to be married.

When Ayesha left, Bubb, in his usual style, berated Mouj again.

'This is your son,' he said to her. 'This is what happens when you raise him without discipline.'

Instead of Mouj's habitual resistance – 'He is your son too!' – she was quiet.

'This is what happens when you give him too much freedom!' he said again. He stood silently at the kitchen counter. 'I have been telling you for years.' Mouj knew what he was talking about. They never said it out loud, as neither had the words to do so. It had been a source of embarrassment for them since he was young, but now that he wanted to be married, it was bound to become even more of a problem.

'How am I supposed to stop that!' Mouj shot back finally. 'It was your job as a father to speak to him about these things.'

'This was the inevitable result of his neglected prayers and fading devotion. You didn't do what I had asked you to do,' Bubb said.

He knew that it was their duty to stop Farooq from indulging in sin. He had hoped that he would grow out of it, as young boys often did. But she was his mother – it should have been easier for her to talk to him, even if it was Bubb's duty to discuss with his son the matters of manhood. He understood why she could not, but he too was helpless.

Farooq finally returned home, greeted them, and asked for dinner. Mouj accompanied Farooq to the kitchen and behaved warmly as usual. Farooq tried to figure out, from Mouj's reactions, what his parents felt about Fatima and what his sister had said to them, but Mouj pretended as if she knew nothing and didn't mention Ayesha's visit either. Things went as normal. They went to sleep.

Farooq went to bed both happy and guilty. In the dark of his room, finally alone, he had surrendered himself to pleasure, a respite from the anxiety of the day. Fatima – would they even let him ask for her hand?

He knew he was a failure, and he knew that his habit was the cause.

Failures followed him everywhere. General daily failures: not getting praise for helping his father in the garden, receiving punishment by the maulvi for not memorising chapters of the Quran, his bony physique. And then there were other, more specific failures like the calf that died a few days after its birth. That one, he had felt, was punishment from a watchful God, after which he had sworn he would stop, but in a few days' time, when he woke up, he had felt the urge again.

That was the morning their cow died, just three days after the calf, just three days after God had punished his family for his filthy habit. The guilt dazed him. He stopped again for a while, but inevitably, he ended up doing it again.

After moving to the clinic, it got worse. He used to stay there from Monday through Saturday, returning to his parents' house on Saturday evening. He shared his room with another colleague and would wait until the weekend to be able to touch himself where nobody could see him. However, one particularly bad day, he could not wait for the weekend – he thought he could do it quickly and silently at night, but his older roommate and colleague caught him. He told everybody the next morning, and they all laughed as his face burned with shame.

An older colleague had seen that he was upset and had come to him later. It was normal, he said, trying to comfort him, and that everyone did it.

It was the first time anybody had told him that – he had believed that he alone suffered in this way and that he was sick for giving in to it so much. He cherished the realisation.

But soon, his father came to visit him at the clinic. 'You've become weak!' he said, frowning at Farooq's clothes. 'Have they not been treating you properly?'

'Him! Weak!' His older roommate laughed out loud. 'He's so weak that he is at it morning, noon, and night!'

He had seen his father's face grow small as he immediately understood what was being insinuated – his father knew, had always known. It was not normal. From that day onwards, he could never talk with his father frankly. He didn't dare to look into his eyes for fear of what he would see. He was sure that Bubb would have told his mother and she knew too. Somehow, nobody ever talked about it; everything remained as it always was – he saw them every weekend when he returned home.

The morning after Ayesha had told them about Fatima, Farooq woke up late and missed his prayers. Bubb had been awake since early dawn as usual, thinking about Farooq, upset at him for being the same – irresponsible and irreligious.

Farooq hesitantly entered the kitchen for breakfast. Mouj was not there. Before he could reach the side of the kitchen where the samovar was placed, his eyes caught sight of Bubb looking straight at him.

Farooq couldn't judge that expression of Bubb; he had always found Bubb's face a little difficult to read. Awkwardly, Farooq moved his hand and got hold of a cup hung on a wooden shelf, the steam coming out from the samovar making a wet path up to the shelf. He hurriedly poured a cup of tea, took a roti from the basket kept adjacent to the samovar and left without saying a word.

'He acts like a child still,' Bubb said to himself, feeling the familiar shame and rage as he watched his son slip out.

Mouj had gone out to the nearest stream right across their house. While standing near the window in his room on the first floor, Farooq saw her carrying the filled pitcher and rushed to help her. He took it from her shoulder and placed it in the kitchen, where he again glanced at Bubb silently; this time, Bubb's face was a mask of rigid disapproval. His lips were pressed into a thin, bloodless line, and his brow furrowed so deeply it shadowed his eyes, which bore into Farooq with unmistakable disgust and contempt.

Farooq quickly ran out without closing the kitchen door this time. Mouj saw him going back to his room. She looked at Bubb, sitting in the baithak, the cosy corner of the kitchen where the family gathered to eat.

'Don't you get tired sitting and doing nothing?' Mouj snapped. 'Go find something to do instead of glaring at everyone.'

Bubb did not respond, and a minute later, she found him smiling grimly.

'You must be happy,' Bubb said with scorn. 'Your son is showing great care for you today. He wants to win you over so that you would support him about that girl.'

Mouj laughed. 'Farooq is everything to me,' she said. 'Of course I will do anything for his happiness, unlike you. I don't see anything wrong in it if he is in love with a Syed girl. That is above all these things – these names and identities.'

'Arey! My malika-e-hayat has become this wise!' Bubb said. 'You think your son is good enough for her!' He was so loud that his voice reached Farooq's room. It left him curious – were his parents talking about his possibilities with Fatima? He tried to listen carefully but heard nothing.

For days he waited, but his parents made no move.

Finally, they got the news: Fatima's family had got her engaged to a teacher.

Bubb tried to make him understand that it was important to be somebody, have a good earning and a reputation in Poshmarg to get what he wanted. A sharp exchange with his parents ended in brittle silence. Shaken but determined, Farooq gathered his things and left for the city, heading back to Dr Jan's clinic. When Farooq went back to the clinic after days of waiting, they told him he had lost his position. In frustration, as a last resort, he went to live with his cousins, across the Valley.

Theirs was a family that made carpets. They sat together for it, and all members of the family became involved. The warp and weft of the weave, the steady rhythm of the loom in his hands – it soothed Farooq more than any comforting word could. When he finally returned home several months later, it was with a faint hope that he might have found something to do that even his parents could respect.

But then came the long night spent in the mosque and everything else that followed it – Farooq, with his broken arm, fleeing with Ayesha, Gul and the baby to the town and what they found upon their return.

***

Nothing mattered then. For the first time in his life Farooq thought he had clarity. He wanted to avenge his parents. His body never fully recovered from the beatings, and as he watched baby Ahmed, he was filled with frustration and worry for his future. He wanted to do something with his rage. He had been punished as though he was a militant – why not, he thought, actually earn the punishment? It was a time when it wasn't difficult to cross the border. He quietly gave word of his desire to a friend of a friend and was contacted swiftly by an undercover agent of a group of freedom fighters.

When he left, he did not know what he should expect. But what he found amazed him. He didn't want to mock the people on the other side for their backwardness, but he couldn't hold his laughter when he was told, 'Look, this is called thermos – tea remains warm in it. You only have samovars, right? Here you'll find modern gadgets you could only dream of in India-Occupied Kashmir.' They too were building castles out of nothing.

Slowly, his rage slipped away, and he found himself lost again. The grass was no greener here than it was at home.

When he finished his training, he was sent back. After a few months of hiding from and playing with the security forces in the city, he got a chance to replace someone from his group who was assigned at Poshmarg.

One night he went to meet Ayesha and Gul. Ayesha stood there crying, her eyes searching his face for the little brother she had known. The soft, boyish edges of his jaw had sharpened into something jagged and stern. In his eyes, the youthful boldness she remembered had been replaced by a quiet, haunted discipline. He was no longer a young man playing at life; the weight of his choices had finally settled into his bones. She was worried for him, and she was angry, she said. The uniformed men had been at their door, again and again, searching for him. They were happy to see him, but they thought he was a fool to have joined the militants.

'Freedom fighters?' Gul said, expressing his disbelief, when Farooq tried to explain himself. 'Where is the freedom? In jail? In the forest? With your parents buried in the ground?'

Farooq didn't want to hear that and regretted his decision of coming to see them. Before he left, he put a note in Ahmed's hands, said prayers for him, kissed his forehead, and left.

Years later, he received a bullet in his left ankle while his two companions were killed just outside Poshmarg in an ambush attack by Indian soldiers. He crawled and hid in the bushes. Struggling to cross back, he waited until it was safe to move.

Somehow he managed to reach the lawns of his cousin's house at the far corner of Poshmarg and asked him not to inform members of the family. It was then that he found out what had happened to Gul.

'Are you sure the militants did it?' he asked. 'They could have been the uniformed men in disguise. How do you know they were not?'

'We don't know for sure,' his cousin said. 'Unknown gunmen.'

Farooq realised then that there was no returning to the life of a gunman; but to stay and help Ayesha and Ahmed, he knew he would have to surrender himself. When he was given four years, he thought to himself: *That's still something. Ahmed would still be young when I get out.* He would be able to help them.

While in jail, he got interested in books. Sindbad, Hayy Ibn Yaqzan, Odysseus, Azad, Amir Hamza, Robinson Crusoe, Gulliver, Hatim Tai, Don Quixote – the lives of these characters became a catalyst for his own, forcing him to embark on a difficult journey of self-discovery and transformation.

The first months were a blur of cold concrete and the sudden violence of the guards. But once the interrogations faded into a dull, routine ache, Farooq found a way to survive. By volunteering for the most menial tasks, he eventually gained access to the prison's workshop. There, amidst the dust and the watchful eyes of the wardens, he found a loom – a wooden skeleton that allowed him to weave his shattered thoughts into something tangible.

After his release, he moved to live with Ayesha. He was a changed man now. Known all over the town as a surrendered militant, he could not go out without feeling shame and avoided it as much as he could. Every morning, he returned to the rhythm of the loom that he had built in Bubb's house. He felt no urge to weave the symmetrical perfections of his childhood. He ignored the talim – the coded scripts of instructions he had once followed like law – and turned away from the traditional designs like hamadan, Tree of Life and the chinar leaf motifs. The intricate, floral geometries that had defined his people for centuries now felt like a cage of silk and wool that he was no longer willing to inhabit; instead he wanted to show what he saw around him, what he had been through.

One day, over breakfast, Ayesha said, 'Did you know that Fatima got divorced?' He looked up at her. 'Yes,' she said. 'While you were away.' He said nothing and continued eating.

The next day, he went to her house. Nothing was going to stop them this time, and she confessed that her feelings for him had been one of the reasons for the divorce. The two found their lost peace again when they finally married.

He began crafting tapestries and rugs that vividly depicted the culture and life in Poshmarg: on one loom, a woman emerged in a pheran of deep plum, her silhouette graceful as she balanced a clay pot atop her head. On another, he captured the steam rising in threads of silver from a tarnished copper samovar, the tea being poured into cups in a golden-amber stream. But the darkness of his past still bled into the wool; he wove a mother cloaked in mourning charcoal, her frame slumped in agony over the ashen face of her fallen son.

As his confidence grew, his palette brightened. He captured the fiery vermilion and copper of chinar leaves in the fall, providing a vibrant backdrop for children chasing a cricket ball through the golden dust of the village square. In his rugs, a line of men knelt in prayer, their backs a rhythmic wave of indigo and cream against the moss-green of the mosque floor. With every piece he sold, the weight of the 'curse' seemed to lift, replaced by the quiet, sturdy certainty of a man who had finally found his way home through the weaves.

In a year, he and Fatima were blessed with a son. They named him Tufail. In Farooq's heart, Ahmed held the place of his first son. It was a sentiment Ahmed mirrored in his own life, growing up to treat Tufail as his younger brother.

Each carpet took him a month to finish, sometimes up to forty days. At times, he accepted advance payments from interested parties; other times, he felt that the middlemen undervalued his work, for they asked him to stick to the tried-and-tested patterns, but he could not.

Slowly he started to make a name for himself, for carpets that were unlike the ones being made and sold in the Valley and started finding clients who would pay for this uniqueness.

Eventually a friend taught him how to sell his carpets directly to customers overseas.

Now the money was enough to keep them together, but his practice meant more to him. There was one carpet he refused to sell, that he finally put in his own home. He had poured into it his dreams.

This carpet, on which Tufail played innocently, seemed to gaze back at him with an air of mystery, as if harbouring countless untold stories.

***

'He must grow up to be a legendary man,' his teachers thought at school.

He spent his life according to a youthful plan.

'What then?' sang Nietzsche's spirit.

What then?

Everything he did was widely received.

He won all – money and fame.

What then?

He could create a space among the greatest artists of his time.

The Man from Kashmir

He played a vital role in liberating his land.
All his dreams came true.
'What then?' repeated Nietzsche's spirit.
What then?
He's a revered spiritual too.
He has, in his hands, both the worlds.
'He surely has a place among the top layers of
Heaven,' thought all his comrades.
But louder sang the spirit,
'What then?'

6

The Wildman

Like everyone else, I believed that the stories about wild creatures, particularly rantas (witch) and wan-mohneu (wildman), were only myths made up to scare children. Until she dragged me here.

The dense trees, the bushes grown over the fallen pines like vultures eating the dead, and the dimness of the deep valley, two mountains too close together – it was where ghosts made home.

'But how did she find you at all?' asked Farooq.

'Yes, why are you here? This is not the part of the forest that we come to. Aren't we all taught that as children?' Ahmed said. 'I came with Farooq mamu because he insisted on looking for some special herb in the dark side of the forest.'

After Ahmed's father had died a few years ago, Farooq had stepped in to become his guardian. Farooq had led Ahmed away for the day, seeking the green refuge of the forest. His only intention was to draw the boy out of the rising storm, a chilling wave of civilian resistance. The days of Ragda were already here, thumping through the very heart of Poshmarg, a tide of protest where youth – including boys like Ahmed – found a release, a sport for freedom in the rhythmic, rallying cry: 'ragdo ragdo…'

They lowered their eyes, stealing glances at the wildman, who was sitting on a big dry log. Farooq and Ahmed were lounging around a big rock beside him.

'I don't know where to start.'

'The beginning,' Farooq said. 'How did you come here?'

'Okay. It was sometime in the winter of 1987 or 1988 – no, 1989. No. I don't remember the exact date. I awoke in the middle of the night. My wife and my little son were fast asleep. I didn't bother to wake them up.'

'Won't you tell us your name? Where did you live?' Farooq asked curiously.

'I forgot to tell you my real name. Wait. I think it is best not to disclose my identity. Call me by any name. I am a common man like everyone else in this forest. I am you. I am this boy.'

'Very well. And then?'

'I went outside and saw that the trees were bent over with snow. A thick white blanket covered my lawn. I took my umbrella in one hand, a lantern in the other and went straight to the cowshed to check if the cow was all right – she was due to give birth soon. She seemed fine, so I locked the cowshed and began walking back. I walked past the apple tree and pulled on one branch to shake the snow off. That's when I heard a woman's voice call out my name. I thought it was my wife and rose to call back, but I stopped. I remembered that I had locked the door from the outside. She was inside the house and would not have been able to hear me.

'The voice called out again. Scared, I tried to find the source of the voice and walked towards the pomegranate tree. There was so much snow on the tree's branches and leaves that the biggest branch had snapped and fallen. As I went closer, I saw what I thought was a woman dressed in white, lying on the ground. She was looking straight at me. "It's an illusion," I thought. "It's just the snow."

'But my hands had begun to shake, and the lantern slipped – the light went out.'

The wildman took a deep breath.

'I realised that whoever she was, she wasn't human. I turned and ran. I could see the door of my house. She was behind me and calling me. "Stop!" she said. I knew I could not, for it would mean the end. My trembling heart, shaky legs, and the deep snow made the little distance appear like a thousand miles. With great effort, I managed to reach the steps of the veranda. I leaned on the railing, panting, trying to catch my breath. I was home, I thought. Safe.'

Ahmed watched the wildman look away. His tears were running into his grizzled beard in a steady, slow drip.

'I went to push open the door, and a massive hand grabbed my left shoulder. I struggled to free myself, but it was no use. When I cried out, a hand grabbed my head and another covered my mouth. I struggled to free myself and managed to kick the door, but the strong hands dragged me back. The smell of her – like death. Rotten things, dead, trapped and decaying. I could see her closely now. She had a hairy face, a vast, dirty, and hairy body with huge breasts and long nails. Her untidy hair fell over her shoulders. I noticed her feet last: they were turned backward. I was terrified.

'She was exactly like the rantas from my grandmother's stories. She used to tell me about her, to distract me whenever I was crying or wanted something I could not have. I feared that she was going to eat me alive. I fought with all my might. I smashed my head on the veranda while trying to free myself. I lost all my strength and began to suspect she had cast a magic spell on me. Helplessly, I let her tie me to her back with her long hair. I wept, screamed for help, but I think I was the only one there to hear my cries. My struggle to escape was of no use.'

'Yes, and then?' asked Ahmed impatiently. When the wildman did not reply, the young man looked at his uncle.

'She brought you to this cave then, didn't she?' Farooq said loudly, hoping to stir the wildman from his thoughts.

'No, not to this cave. All the way I was unconscious while hitched to her back. I think she walked very fast. Later, when I opened my eyes, I wondered where I was. The place I found myself in was dimly lit. I could see stones and some dry logs, lots of straw, and some sand too. I walked a few steps, exploring the place. A rotten stench floated around; I had to cover my nose and mouth. I found that I was standing upon a large carcass, surrounded by bones. I was frightened, much more than you two were when you first laid eyes on me. "So this is it," I thought to myself. "I am her food." I could see my death.'

'Wasn't she there?' asked Ahmed.

'No, I didn't see her there at that time. I kept searching for a way to escape. But all I could find were little holes in the cave's walls. It was the only source of light in the darkness. I whispered some verses of the Quran and cried, "Mouji, Mouji." I begged God to save me. *What wrong have I done, Allah? How can You end my existence here? Is a grave and a proper funeral not in my fate? I prayed to You regularly, always tried to do good, never committed any grave sin, and this is what You have in store for me? Do I really deserve this? What will happen to my family, my old father and mother, my wife, my son, my little sister, and my brother?*

'Then I saw a big rock turning, and there she was. I kept reciting, "La Ilaha Illallah Mohammad-ur-Rasullullah." She entered and pushed the rock back to close the cave. I said to myself: *Look at her, see her power, she can move mountains, and she may have eaten half the world already. You are just a tiny morsel for her.* As she began to walk towards me, I could hear my heart pounding. It was the first time I had felt so helpless. I begged her. With tears in my eyes, I fell to my knees and begged, "Don't eat me." To my utter surprise, she laughed. It was a burst of strange laughter. I can't describe its musicality. She said that she wouldn't eat her husband and dropped some roots and herbs in front of me. I froze.

'How could I be her husband? Had I heard her right? Had she really said that I was her husband? As I looked at her, all I could do was think about my future. But when I found thinking to be no escape, I slid into remembering things that always gave me pleasure and filled me with joy – my family, their love for me. Moments later, it was as though I had slipped out of my trance. To my utter surprise, I saw my wife in the cave, sitting close to me.'

The wildman began to sob.

Farooq and Ahmed looked at each other, wondering how to respond. 'Khudai kari sahal. God will make things easy for you, and everything will be all right now. It was His will that led us to this side of the forest today,' Farooq said as he tried to console the monstrous wildman sitting before him, crying like a child. 'It seems God was guiding us to you, to save you.'

The wildman sighed.

'Is God still there? I don't believe in Him, Her, Whatever any more!'

'Tell us what happened then. How had your wife arrived there?' asked Farooq.

'I was terrified for her when I saw her there – the first thing I said was that she should run, before asking if the rantas had caught her too. I reached out to touch her hand, but it felt wrong. My wife's hands were soft. She looked at our hands touching then looked back up at me and changed her face before my eyes, going back to being the rantas. She was laughing, delighted with me or with herself, I couldn't tell. "You can be my husband," she said. "I will love you, and you will love me, and I will wear a face that you can love, and you will give me babies." I had to stop myself from vomiting.'

He took a brief pause before continuing, 'You will find that when faced with the possibility of being killed, a man will do almost anything.'

Farooq started to say something, and then stopped, troubled. He gave a concerned look to Ahmed.

'Eventually, I didn't even have to worry about being killed. My fears started to fade away. I learned to talk to her, and it was easier to love her when she disguised herself as Lalie. Stupid me! See I couldn't hide the name of my wife. But when I woke up in the morning and found myself on top of her undisguised, bare self, her fetid smell in my nostrils, I would want to kill her, and myself. But I couldn't. I think she knew what I was thinking, and it just made her laugh. She liked it when I fought. So I stopped thinking of it. Mystifying as it was, it was my reality. I accepted that I had become a wan-mohneu, a wildman.'

He was strangely calm. His eyes bore into Ahmed's.

'Tell me, what's the date today? I remember the days of the week. In the early days of my captivity, I would count them, but then I stopped. There was no point. I can only guess that many ages have passed by now.'

Ahmed looked away from the wildman and at his mobile phone. He noticed there was no network coverage. 'It's Monday, 11 August. 12.25 p.m.'

'Which year?'

'2008.'

He jerked back. 'What! Are you serious? No, it cannot be. Have I spent this much time here! I don't accept it. No, it is not true. God, what have you done to me?'

Farooq said, 'Don't you see yourself? You hardly look human. When we first saw you, we thought you were some creature of the jungle. If you hadn't called out to us, we would never have come to you. Come with us. Let's go. Now. You'll be a great surprise to your family.'

The wildman remained silent. When the young man insisted that he reply, he spoke harshly: 'No, I can't leave. I have three daughters here.'

'O may lightning fall on you!' Ahmed uttered, shocked.

'How's it possible? Where are they?' Farooq asked.

'They have gone to get food. They only spend their nights in this cave. You should leave me here. You don't know what they would do to you if they saw you here.'

Farooq leaped up and shouted, 'You fool! Why did you not tell us this before! How long have you kept us here! And why do you still want to stay with them when you could easily escape with us?'

'They will find us easily if I go away with you. I won't endanger your lives,' he said. 'I keep watch from the holes in my cave. I haven't seen another human here in… decades. I didn't know if I should call you. I couldn't stop myself. I think you might be the last human faces I will ever see.' Tears coursed down his cheeks again and disappeared into his long bushy beard.

'But I have to remain calm and stay inside this cave. You are very courageous for coming here and listening to me, but please be careful. A long time ago, when my daughters were little, and we lived in another cave, I watched three men with their long axes, just like yours, approach the cave. When I called out to them, they came to help me. When they peeped through the stones and saw me, they ran away, screaming. My face probably frightened them. They didn't even look back. I know I look like a monster – my long dirty hair, my beard, my nails, and my foul smell. As you can see, I am an old wildman now. Once I realised there was no way out of here, nothing else mattered – not how I spoke or looked. I was without hope and adopting her ways of life seemed like the best recourse.

'We also had two sons, but they didn't survive. She can't have sons because her clan is cursed. She is the last fully grown rantas left in this forest.'

Farooq scratched his head and looked at Ahmed, who seemed lost. It was as if he had fallen into a pit of secrets – or as if the wildman had bewitched him. Farooq's face lost colour as the thought came to him; he sturdily held the axe. He moved closer to Ahmed and pointed to his watch, but Ahmed was still in a daze. When Ahmed still didn't see him, Farooq raised his voice: 'So are we going to stay here, in this cave?'

'Forgive me. It is because I have so much to tell. Yes, you should leave now. I am thankful to you for allowing me to feel like a human again,' the wildman said quietly.

'We will come again with more men soon, don't lose hope,' Farooq replied. 'Where are you from? We will inform your family about you.'

'I don't remember. Even if I did, I couldn't tell you much about me. And please don't tell anyone else about me either. Go straight to your home. Be careful.'

Before leaving, Farooq paused for a moment. The thought of passing on his long axe to the wildman came to his mind. He checked the impulse, and the next thought stayed his hand. However, he offered a final instruction: 'Live without fear.'

***

As soon as they had moved away from the cave, Farooq turned towards Ahmed. 'Why was he looking only at you, at your eyes? He was staring at you even as we left. I feel afraid. He could be looking for someone who can replace him. He must be worried about his daughters. And why wouldn't he tell us about his home?'

'Mamu, don't worry. The poor man lives in another world. He looks frightening, but his story touched my heart. I think we should come back with more men and save him. I can't bear to think of him waiting for us, hoping we'd keep our promise, as the years go by.'

The two carefully walked in the forest, searching for a path that would take them back to their friends.

The group of woodcutters had been looking for them for many hours. Unable to find them, they finally gathered around a clump of trees. They were nervous. Frightened, they had been trying, again and again, to contact them, but there was no network coverage. Suddenly, one of them shouted: 'There they are! Captain Farooq and his little dog Ahmed.' The men jumped with joy.

'What should we tell them when they ask us where we were?' Ahmed whispered to Farooq as they walked towards their group.

'They are our own men,' Farooq answered. 'We aren't supposed to hide anything from them. See how happy they are to see us. They must have been searching for us. There's love in their concern.'

***

They began to walk together through the forest towards their residences. Habib-ul-Lah, the group leader, asked Farooq about his and Ahmed's disappearance, but before Farooq could answer, another man in their group yelled, 'Why don't you tell them what they've missed? Tell them what we did!'

'After lunch, when you both disappeared, Ustaad Habib-ul-Lah asked us to look for you,' Aijaz, Farooq's friend, narrated. 'We searched the places you usually go to but couldn't find you. For a moment, we thought you had joined the protest march. But then we realised there was not any rally happening this side. We came back, and Ustaad gave us his gun. Akram, Sultan, Yousuf, and I took our axes and a few other essential things and went to the dark side of the forest. We climbed up the hill to see if we could catch a glimpse of you two from the top.

'But – and you must believe us, Ahmed, Farooq – we saw the witch of the woods. She was exactly like they had told us she would be when we were small. Huge, giant woman, naked in the snow, covered in hair and shit.

'"Rantas, rantas, Khudaya…" Yousuf began to shout.

'We were frightened. We thought both of you might be dead. I wanted to run back, but you know Akram and Sultan. They wanted to find you both, so we had to confirm you were not still hiding if she had not got to you. We moved slowly until we reached her nest. She had made a nest by joining the fallen branches and trunks and using dry logs to make the bed frame. She had layered the bed with dry leaves.

'We looked around for you, carefully. We could hear her snoring. As we were about to leave, Akram whispered something to Sultan and raised the gun he was carrying. The two of them walked silently towards her. Rantas slept peacefully in the hot sun. We hid behind the pines. Akram had carried some concertina wire – he had found it around that old uniformed men's camp on the other side of the forest. He tied it around her and wedged it between the big logs. We didn't want her to be able to get up when we made the pyre around her. She barely moved; she was sleeping so deeply. We moved like we were in a trance. When we lit the pyre, the witch was still fast asleep, but as the dry logs and leaves underneath and around her started burning, we heard her scream.'

'Oh God,' Ahmed whispered. 'You've killed the witch.'

Then Farooq told them about their encounter with the wildman.

After listening to Farooq's story, Habib-ul-Lah said, 'You fools! You were foolish to stay there, even for a moment.' He was known for his valour – he had once chopped off the little finger of his left hand after a snakebite. He told them about the legend of wan-mohneu, and his power to enchant women.

'One evening, around three years ago, a young man came to me and asked for help. His wife was in danger. My friend and I agreed to accompany the young man. We saw his wife walking ahead of us, but she didn't respond when he called out to her. We thought that they had been in a fight and that she was angry and had left her home. So we rushed towards her. That's when we saw the wildman; he was walking a few feet ahead of her. We were only a few steps away from the young woman. It was clear that he had her under a spell, for when we called out to her, asking her to turn back, she didn't respond. Instead, she continued to follow the wildman. When her husband urged her to stop, she replied,

"Leave me. You are no one to me. I am going to live with my real husband or else I will die."

'The young man begged the wildman to release her from his thrall, but he wouldn't listen, and he continued to walk away with the woman following him. When, after all our entreaties, he realised his wife wouldn't come back and she was lost to herself, he took the gun out of my hands and shot her in the back of her head. Then the wildman started to come after us and we ran away. The young man tried to shoot him too. After we had escaped from there, the young man told us how he had been recently married, and his wife had been behaving strangely and had gone missing many times since their wedding.'

Farooq was puzzled. 'Our wildman was just old and lonely. Desperate.'

'I am sure he is the same wildman who was in the news last year,' Sultan chimed in. 'Don't you remember? That French tourist girl went missing. Haven't you heard about that? It was the biggest news last winter. She was skiing in the hills, and there he was. He cast his magic on her, and she willingly followed him into the dense forests. When some people saw her following the wildman, they tried to save her, but she vanished from their sight.'

Farooq looked at Ahmed. Ahmed, too, was in shock. 'He cannot be that,' Ahmed said, 'or else he would not have spared us. He was kind to us.'

Habib-ul-Lah patted Ahmed's shoulder. 'You have a lot to learn, son. Just forget about that wildman.'

He turned to Farooq. 'Ahmed should be careful and strong, and never ever visit that cave again.'

Habib-ul-Lah untied an amulet that was wrapped on his upper arm and transferred its silent vow of protection to Ahmed by securing it around his neck.

'Keep this with you, son. Always.'

***

In the cave, the wildman sat lost in reverie. He thought about his journey from being a God-fearing man to turning into this – a brute, devoid of real guilt, who still wore the clothes of human shame. These were his sins, he thought, and they destroyed both his families. In the past, he used to think about his old family all the time.

He had imagined every possible scenario that could have happened to them. At the beginning of his captivity, he was obsessed with thinking about his family. Later, his dreams about them filled him with pain and anxiety, but they gave him some comfort too. In one dream, he saw his father got Lalie and his younger brother married, but his son didn't like his uncle as his new father.

In another dream, he saw his family living happily with his brother. In the beginning, he often had hallucinations about their cries – the nightmare where, after his father's death, his brother became the sole owner of their property and banished Lalie. When Lalie, along with their son, decided to stay with her family, her brothers too ill-treated them. In a fit of rage, his son killed his uncle in a scuffle and was put in jail. After a few days, the uncle's wife killed Lalie. These nightmares depressed him and chased him ceaselessly.

He could never know what really happened to his family after he was gone. Perhaps they believed he was dead. Probably, Lalie married someone else and was happy. He often thought about his son – his smiling face, his dream to be a rich man, his voice and how he called him Abbu. He wondered if he missed his father.

He came out of his reverie when his daughters entered the cave. Late at night, when the rantas – Kashmira, he called her now – would not come back, he would try to ask about her, but his daughters would remain unbothered. They thought of him as their man, their husband, and of their mother as their competitor. To have a family like everyone else was Kashmira's dream, and it only remained a dream.

'Perhaps she has left me for our daughters,' he thought. He felt as if he had lost his world again. He hated that he felt like this – but Kashmira had warmed his bed for decades, and the love she bore for him was animal. Perhaps it was that she was the only one left who also remembered Lalie's face and still on occasion wore it before they lay together – he never knew why.

It humiliated him to think of sleeping with his own daughters. He remembered how Kashmira had slaughtered the woman whom he, by his magic, had made his slave. All he wanted was a little tenderness. He had missed it, and he knew that no human woman would ever look upon him with anything but horror in her eyes. He couldn't bear it. He would never forget her screams – as his daughters tore apart her naked body. As they set upon her with their teeth, their mouths bloody. The enchantment still at work, the French woman had stared at him while life seeped out of her.

He remembered well his promise to Kashmira – he wouldn't lure any woman again. He could not hurt his children like that again, she had said. She was the one who had given him the gift of his enchantment, and she was the one to take it away. As his daughters grunted into their sleeping corners for the night, he stared into the light slowly dimming from the holes inside his cave.

God, why have you forsaken me – turned me into a monster and abandoned me? How should I keep my faith like this? How do I remember your presence in this deep loneliness? Perhaps you were never there – you never existed – and I was always alone. You gave me two families, and both are broken now because of me! Don't you see I am an old man? I cannot keep on. There is a young man now, walking in my trees. He still has his spirit. He can heal my family and make it whole once more. He is my last hope. Send him here, my lord. Hear my cry, the last breath of my belief. If You could do it, I'll die a believer. If you cannot, we must all die alone.

7
Nowhere Valley

It was a chilly winter morning. Big flakes of snow were swirling lazily and lying in a thin, soft layer on the ground, roofs, trees, and wherever else the eyes went. It was as if the whole world was painted white.

Farooq and Fatima sat in the kitchen, sipping the hot salt tea from the samovar, talking in their quiet voices used only for each other – the little problems of their daily life, the outrage of a long, dull winter. The cold had made them sit there for longer than they usually did, emptying teacup after teacup.

'Is Tufail still sleeping?' Farooq asked. Due to his poor health and eyesight, Farooq had been unable to work on his carpets for a long time.

'Yes, let him sleep. He's your son, truly – he was up reading all night,' Fatima said.

'Don't you think he's becoming more idle day by day?'

'Why are you being so harsh? He is looking for work. He gets so upset if you are disappointed with him.'

'I am not being harsh, Fatima. You know our condition. It is not easy to run a home with barely filled pockets. And he is almost twenty-three now.'

'Everything will be fine,' Fatima said. 'Has God not looked after us so far? It will be all right. The Rehbar-e-Taleem teaching post in our mohalla is, without doubt, Tufail's by right. The position is already reserved for him in the community's mind. There is simply no one else with comparable qualifications.'

Farooq looked at his wife, still beautiful after all this time, even with the lines near her eyes.

They were not wealthy, and they had high hopes from their son. They were desperate to see him settled, to raise and play with his children. Their world, of which their son was the centre, seemed endless. Given the little money they earned from a few looms they still had and their growing age, they would soon become more dependent on him, but they worked hard to give the impression that they would not.

They didn't want their son to feel trapped by responsibilities. They wanted him to live a life of his own and develop himself to his own standards. He was a caring and sensible boy, but they were often worried that he felt pressured and lonely. Their only son – his two brothers had died in their infancy. Despite the meagre income they earned from carpet making, in times when there was no demand for homemade carpets, they were proud to have accomplished the goals of parenthood and give him a good education.

Yes, they were worried. But when they looked at his laughing face or when a neighbour spoke approvingly of him, nothing else mattered.

Tufail was lying still in bed, lost in dreaming with his open eyes about his life and the day that lay ahead. He glanced at his wall clock and jumped out of bed. He went to the window and blinked – the world had turned white overnight. He grumbled to himself while drawing open the windows of his room – the snow was going to make his day much harder.

After morning prayers, he went straight to the kitchen to have breakfast and broke the news to his parents: he had a job interview that day. Though he didn't want to work in the private sector, he did need to make money some way. The day before he had received a call for an interview for a job in a small private company. He was wary of pinning his hopes on this prospect, because of his many disappointments, but his parents were delighted. He didn't want to share this news with his parents because it hurt him when he let them down, and he didn't want to hide anything from them either.

That morning, they loved him a little more. For a second, he thought of staying home and avoiding the risk of the snow, but looking at his mother resolved against it.

After a moment, the snowfall stopped; he put on his favourite jacket and jeans and got ready. His mother stood at the door to give him an umbrella, but he refused to take it. While stepping outside his house, on his way to the main road, he saw the snow covering the entire local road. There was almost no trace of any vehicle or human footprints.

'The main highway should be clear,' he thought. He didn't like going out in the snow. Looking at the different shades of white, the dream from the morning revisited him: he had bought his parents a big house. They were sitting there, as they did here, in the kitchen by the samovar, but their eyes looked bright and happy. When he had woken up, their happiness had lingered in him for a second before reality had asserted itself.

He reached the bus stop, where some people were waiting – some holding umbrellas in their hands and some in local pherans and some, like Tufail, in jackets. He, as usual, hid his disquietude beneath his smiling, shining face.

'Tufail!' a voice cried. He turned around and saw Ahmed.

'Come to this side, where are you going?' asked Ahmed, who was also waiting there.

'The city,' he answered with a smile while getting closer to him to shake his hand and give him a hug.

'Everything okay?'

'Yes yes. An interview.'

'Again!' Ahmed exclaimed.

'Get lucky this time?'

'In sha Allah, you have my prayers!'

Meanwhile, an empty coach stopped for them, and they got in. Ahmed offered the window seat to Tufail.

Tufail resisted. 'You sit on that side, and I'll sit here.'

'Come on, I know you are a man now, but you'll always be my little brother, so get in here.' Ahmed pushed him tenderly with a smile on his face.

Tufail guessed Ahmed must have had some work at the university, applying for certificates and the like, he knew he was trying for international fellowships to study abroad, so he didn't find the need to ask him where he had to go. 'How's Phuphi?' Tufail asked to strike a conversation.

'Alhamdulillah, she's well. Where have you been all this week?' Ahmed asked warmly.

'Home only. You know what happened last week. Abu didn't want me to leave the house.'

'That dead body. It was horrible. Yes, one has to be more careful during election times.'

While on the road, some people travelling with them joined in their discussion about the volatile political atmosphere in Poshmarg. Seated opposite them, a young man wearing a black jacket and sporting a shaved face, blamed the six per cent people of the city for voting, for giving in – those were responsible for choosing an authority to control us here, he said. This was reiterated by an old man in a plain suit, who emphasised how youngsters did not know much about Poshmarg's past – how they were forcefully taken to polling booths for casting votes and were beaten by uniformed men if they didn't have a blue mark on their finger. Now when people did not see hope for resolution, they voted for the basic requirements of life: 'We don't have electricity in winters, we don't have clean water, we don't have good roads, people are getting killed for no reason…'

The driver gave Ahmed a hollow, sideways glance, and he didn't dare to turn on the music.

'Everything is political here,' Tufail added, but Ahmed waved at Tufail to stay silent when he saw the debate becoming more serious. Tufail engaged himself in the scenes outside the window – a play between the sun and snow.

Listening to all those voices, Ahmed felt emotionless, silent. He knew the people would judge him if he opened his mouth. Given that his father was killed by unknown gunmen, Ayesha asked him to be careful, always. She didn't want any labels for Ahmed. But was it really possible to live silently in Poshmarg? As he thought about his homeland, his shiny smiling face turned thoughtful. The other faces present looked more severe than the statues of Greek philosophers.

The discussion drew to an abrupt halt when the bus lurched to the side of the road. Fortunately, it was a little slip, and the driver assured them not to worry – the road was covered with the first snow, so this was expected.

Tufail and Ahmed got off the bus in the city. Ahmed, catching Tufail's arm and chiding him when he tried to get his wallet, gave the fare to the driver. They decided to go on foot. Walking on the road's right side, Ahmed suggested they cross to the other side.

'No, I always walk on the right side,' Tufail said.

'But this is the wrong side, we are supposed to walk on the left,' Ahmed stressed.

'Walking on the right side is better because you watch the cars coming and can move aside. If you're walking on the left in this snow – and with the cars coming from behind – it's too risky during winters on slippery roads.'

'Oh yes, then, it may be right when there's snow,' Ahmed said.

In a few minutes, Tufail saw the signboard of the building where he was expected for the interview. Ahmed asked him if he had enough money, Tufail reassured him that he had enough. Ahmed bid him good luck as Tufail entered the building.

Tufail quickly smoothed his hair, unzipped his jacket, and checked that his shirt was tucked in properly. He took a deep breath.

As he walked inside the office, his eye was drawn to a notice pinned on a wall right beside the door. He moved closer to read it. It was the application notice, which now said 'Vacancies closed' with two names beside it – the people who had been selected.

Trembling with anger, he went to the office room, where he was informed that they were ordered by their chief to cancel the interview.

'What! What are you saying, sir?' Tufail questioned them angrily.

'We are so sorry. The owner of this office, those two boys are his cousin brother's relatives. He could not say no,' the manager said.

'Then what was the point of calling me here? You know how risky it is to travel during this strike and the snow?'

'Sorry! To be honest, we wanted to have you here, but – the owner told us about the boys only this morning. We are helpless.'

The misery which had eased for a short while came back to him and tore at his heart more cruelly than ever. 'What do I do? What will I tell my parents now? No good! I'm no good!' he kept repeating to himself as he walked out of the office.

He came out of the shock when a jeep swiftly passed by him on the road filled with snow water, and the water hit his shoes. His hands, unwillingly but instinctively, checked his pockets for his wallet, to see if he was carrying his identity card.

The jeep stopped ahead of him, and suddenly, he was being frisked. While they questioned him, an old man walked up to them. He had seen

Tufail with uniformed men from a little distance and limped quickly in their direction, moving by the support of a stick.

'Ho, gobra!' he cried as he neared them. 'Can't slow down for this old uncle?' He smiled benevolently at the uniformed men, who, suddenly self-conscious, let go of Tufail and got back into their jeep.

Tufail stammered his thanks to the man and swiftly tried to cross the street, an urgent need to get away from that spot.

The old man called him to stop. Tufail stopped and waited for him while he crossed the road. 'I was sure they would have taken you,' the old man said.

'I was just walking,' Tufail said, still recovering from the shock.

'Yes,' the man said. 'That was enough.'

While they walked, he asked Tufail to introduce himself. Tufail found it a little odd, but he understood the old man's sincerity and told him about himself.

'I was a lecturer in the education department, retired a few months ago,' the old man responded.

Tufail fumbled – he had thought of him as an eccentric nobody but now thought it better to change the register of his speech and be more respectful.

'You know, when we were young, jobs were not so hard to come by. I feel bad for your generation – what will you boys do like this? What future is here? But don't worry! God has something great in store for you too. Don't give up hope.' The old lecturer seemed concerned about the youngsters of Kashmir.

He was the one who, Tufail thought, had finally read and understood his anxiety. Although Tufail was a bit shy, and usually didn't talk much, he opened up to this old man.

The man kept talking as they walked down Amira Kadal.

'You remind me of my little boy,' he told Tufail.

'Me! How, sir?' Tufail wondered if his son was also job hunting. 'He looked like you. Same height. Character too, I think.'

'Where is he, sir?'

Wistfulness veiled his friendly face. The old man shook his head and continued: 'He always loved to read. He would read until late in the night, and he wanted to be a doctor. So he was preparing for the MBBS entrance test.' He stopped and took a deep breath.

'One morning he asked me for some money – he had some applications. I went to my high school as usual. When I came home, he had not come back. We waited; thought it was traffic, but it wasn't like him not to call us.' He stopped again and looked into the distance, his face still closed. 'He was sensitive. Knew his mother would worry.'

'By evening, there was no electricity either, so my late father played Sheharbeen on the radio, and we heard the news. Some grenade blast, in the main chowk. My brother borrowed someone's car, and we went with a neighbour. They kept telling me he would be okay, but my heart was already weeping. Some uniformed men stopped us at the bypass, and we had to beg them – I had to beg them – "Please, my son might be at the police station. He might be at the morgue," I pleaded to them. They took us there themselves then, but he was not there, with the bodies.'

He stopped again. Tufail wondered where this story was going – he had braced himself to hear of an unpleasant death, but it did not seem to be coming.

The old man continued. 'The police didn't let us leave to check the hospital – to this day I don't know why. We spent the night there, sitting on the floor of the police station. Couldn't sleep. In the morning, when they let us go – we did not find him at the hospital either.'

He stopped. 'I haven't seen him since that day. There is nowhere we have not looked.'

Tufail was filled with an unfamiliar emotion – half sorrow, half guilt. He had the urge to leave, walk away from this man and the ghost of his son as quickly as possible.

When they reached the bus station, the man turned to him.

'Can we meet again, son? I would like to know how things go with you.'

Tufail's words were caught in his mouth. He could not say no, but he could not bring himself to say yes either, to lie to this man when he knew he would never want to meet him again.

'It's just that … it feels like I met him again,' the old man said, now looking at him with open desperation. 'My son. I live with my daughter now.'

'Of course, sir,' Tufail said, his tongue finally loosened.

Tufail saved his phone number on the mobile phone of the old man.

'It will be my pleasure, sir, if I can be of any help to you,' Tufail said while leaving, the old man blessing him as he went.

As he sat in the bus, the thought of the old man's son would not leave him. What if his son was alive and returned to his family? It would be startling. *This man is poorer than my parents! What if I had joined the revolutionaries? I would have escaped the mundane responsibilities of this life.*

He thought of the unspoken thing lingering in the air, the place the father would not look at and where he could not look away from. After all, had he not done the same thing – borrowed money one morning and simply not come back? He looked out of the window. He wondered if his mother had gone to the morgue too, looking into the strange faces of other people's sons to find her own. She didn't have a daughter to look after her either; it would have just been the two of them, holding on to each other in front of their samovar, waiting for him to come back home.

He reached home and stepped inside, shaking the snow off his shoes. His mother, who was waiting for him, called out to him – he had come back just in time to have lunch, she said. Though it was not lunchtime – it was time for tea – she always wanted Tufail to eat a full meal.

Tufail thought of the day that he had not come home. The day he went so heroically to join the resistance, he thought to himself, there must have been lunch on the table, growing cold. He thought of the day his parents finally spotted him, almost a month later, in a hamlet near the Line of Control, far away from their home. He thought of how far they would have had to come to reach there, and how they looked.

He wore his pheran and came to the kitchen, where his mother had already put a plate of rice, his favourite dal in a bowl and vegetable pickle along with a glass of milk and a glass of boiled water on a cloth sheet.

'My dear, you must be hungry. Eat all this rice,' his mother said to him.

'Where is Abu?' Tufail asked.

'He's outside in the backyard. How was your interview?'

Tufail dropped his head down, looking at his food, and was silent. His mother's heart sank.

Farooq saw his son as he came into the house, but did not sense the tension in the room.

'Well?' he said beaming. 'Tell us the good news?'

'I didn't get it, Abu,' Tufail said, sounding defeated. 'There were two boys – the owner's relatives. They got it before I even entered the door.'

His father came to stand beside him and put his hand on his shoulder, looking out of the window. He tried to remind him that there was hope that God had intended for something good to come out of this too. 'Khudayan aasi ath manz te rut thovmut!' he said.

'There is no guarantee in these small private jobs,' he continued after a pause, 'they pay so little, and they make you work until night. Don't worry! You deserve better. You'll get a government job soon, in sha Allah. Fatima, give him some more food.' His mother hurried to add some more rice to his plate.

There was a tightness in Tufail's throat.

After dinner, Tufail, as usual, locked the outer gate of his home before going to bed. In the snow-light, he saw some men coming to their lane. In the snow-light, it was impossible to know who they were. He dashed into his house, locked the door and asked his parents to sleep. The house was silent.

His father looked at him, standing by the window, unmoving. 'They won't come here, Tufail. Remember what the commander said – "The greatest jihad is to look after your old parents." Sleep now. Tomorrow is a strike again.'

Tufail lay down in his bed, eyes climbing over the interlocked wood of the ceiling. Sleep remained elusive. It was his birthday, his birth hour, 11.25 p.m. He opened a diary and wrote:

These days,
The night comes early,
The lights don't come on,
The ground does not sing,

The Man from Kashmir

Trees stand with bare arms in this cold,
Even rain is too scared to come home,
Let alone snow.
When our name on the lips of hollow liberals,
Is as loud as our speech is silent,
When the calendars are marked,
With the end of our days.
When we are tired,
When we are tired,
A boy walks up to a red door,
He has not learned to be afraid,
Please, he says to the gun,
It's my birthday.

Can we strike tomorrow instead?
He walks away,
Hot tears in the cold,
Freezing on his face.

Who will come?
Who will come for me?
Will he save us in the camp?
Will he save us in the snow?
And will he manage to hold me
Before the cold ground does?

8

Hope and Fear

Fatima left. She took with her all the delight of her family.

Fatima was no longer worried about the fresh wrinkles and sagging under her sad eyes, which she had noticed in the mirror before leaving for hospital. Her fallen face, layered with bitterness, anguish and fear, made her family more worried for her.

Without thinking how they would react, she contacted a private travel company, paid extra money and booked herself for an umrah starting the next month.

When Farooq and Tufail came to know about it, they were first bewildered, and after she refused to attend to their confusion, were infuriated.

Why was Fatima – a good wife and a good mother – suddenly behaving so out of character?

Farooq, her husband, tried to find out what was wrong with her. 'Has she committed any grave sin?' he wondered. 'No, she cannot do that.' It was unimaginable. He had no reason to doubt her loyalty. He had always felt blessed to have her in his life. Farooq tried to talk to her, but she simply changed the subject each time without giving him an answer, and if he pressed a little more, she just said, 'I must.'

Farooq wondered whether she was travelling with some of her friends and reached out to them quietly to ask. They were puzzled by the question – no, they were not travelling with her, and more importantly, why would she not have told her husband? He would end these conversations with a swift laugh, trying to smoothen the awkwardness with a casual note. No one was happy with her decision to travel alone with strangers. Farooq pleaded with her – they would apply for the following year's Haj and go together. But she refused even that. She was without anger, and did not seem perturbed, but would not be moved.

They tried to convince her first with coaxing, then with frustration – it was not common for a woman to go for umrah alone! She was acting as though she had no family; look how Farooq was being so reasonable too. After days of this, nobody could speak to her in the usual tone; every word they spoke with her was heavy with frustration and disappointment.

Until then, she had never done anything that was against the wishes of her family. Something inside her was haunting her, and that had twisted her behaviour. But nobody in her family could be told. As the day scheduled for her pilgrimage came nearer, her family surrendered their fury. After all, this was her first time going against their desires – even in that, it was for a religious calling. They supported her. They didn't want her to feel alone. Besides what else could they do? They accompanied her when she went to meet all their relatives and friends, as is customary for all the Muslims who are to take on the holy pilgrimage: to ask for forgiveness and blessings, to visit the sacred land with pure spirit.

Slowly they noticed that she was broken inside. They would find her weeping whenever she met people, and when she asked them to forgive her, it felt as though it were an urgent, real matter, not one of ritual. Some of them found this distasteful – her weeping would often seem excessive, and some even wondered if it was just her way of getting the attention she thought was her due.

Others felt that something was wrong but didn't dare to discuss it with her. Farooq bought and packed everything she would need, met with the other people who were going with her, ensured her safety, and they had a big feast on the night of her departure.

Fatima knew they pretended to be pleased before their neighbours, relatives, and even with her. She wanted to make them feel good, but she was deliberately trying to make them despise her.

It would be easier for them, she thought. Not to be burdened by their love for her, if she could not even care for them.

They accompanied her to the airport. No matter how hard she tried, she could not hold back her tears when her husband held her for the last time before she left. She had to smile through it, to tell her son that everything would be all right. She could see the bewilderment in her husband's eyes; they had been together for long enough that he knew she was in pain, that she did not want this, but would do it nonetheless. As he saw her preparing to leave, he had to make his heart grow cold, so he would not say the words that were fighting to come out of his mouth senselessly. *Why are you leaving us? Do not leave us. Do not leave me.* She was coming back, after all.

Farooq took a deep breath and put on the mask of happiness, of casual indifference. If she wanted to go, she could go.

'Come, Tufail,' he said abruptly to his son. 'Don't keep your mother any longer.'

Fatima looked at him, and then away. She wanted to talk to him with love, but to do that she would need to let him in, and she could not. Her voice was brittle when she bid her goodbyes; she did not look back when she walked away.

The journey was tiring; somehow, she managed to reach Madinah.

On getting there, she was amazed at seeing the holy city she had desired to visit all her life. Mainly when she was in Mecca, she was both proud and embarrassed: proud to be a Muslim and witness the glory of Islam and embarrassed by her own loneliness; it was a fate left for widows, and here she was, willingly keeping her family away from herself to do it. For a moment she felt an overpowering urge to go back, to bring them here, to be the whole of herself – mother, daughter, wife, woman. She shut her eyes tightly and prayed for each of them by name.

Momentarily, she thought about the purpose of her visit. Perhaps she would die here and that would be good – the best. It was all she wanted: either a blessed death or a cure for her deadly disease.

How could she tell them, after all, that the cancer was there, rooted deep within her, that it would stay until it ate her away? They would be wretched. Bereft. A mourning would be upon them before death arrived.

This way at least she could ensure a little peace before the sorrow that was looming in front of them inched closer and engulfed them. And if not that what if they were consumed by the indignity of hope? Their savings were for their son's future; what if they decided to spend it on her present? After all, cancer came without guarantees. It was an unreasonable risk – her life in exchange for her son's.

She spent her days performing rituals and prayers. She wanted to recite the name of Allah with every breath she inhaled. Death, she prayed, or cure. She could not go back without this. She spoke to God, trembled as she screamed silently inside her mind, hammering at His doors. Death or cure. I will not go back without one of these. By the time she had finished her final cycle of prayers, the strength was sapped from her, and she went to lie in her bed, exhaustion weighing down her limbs. It would be tonight, she thought to herself grimly. He would listen and make His judgment tonight.

The next morning, she woke up.

The sun filtered gently through the curtains, and she held up her fingers, skin almost translucent in the light, and watched the blood beat inside her hands. Death or cure. It was not death, so it must have been cure. She moved almost as in a dream, suffused with peace, clarity and joy, as she made her preparations to return. Her prayers had been answered. She could go home now.

When she reached the airport, Tufail ran up to her as soon as he saw her at the gate. Her husband walked sedately behind him, his eyes scanning her uncertainly. 'So?' he said. 'You're back...'

'I am back,' she said. She looked at him directly, and the joy in her eyes met his like a promise.

Something in him eased – his wife had returned to him.

Once they were home, their each movement felt like it was infused with love. When his relatives pressed him on why he hadn't accompanied her on the pilgrimage, he would say, 'My wife is a godly woman, and she listened to God even when I could not. She is a gift to us,' and the simplicity of the pride in his eyes, shining through without hesitation, quietened their doubts. When they left, it was with a feeling that they had been in the presence of grace.

After one month, Fatima got a call; it was from her oncologist's office, to schedule her next appointment. She laughed on the phone. 'I'll come,' she said, 'but you won't find anything.' She wondered for a minute whether getting herself checked was like spitting in the face of God to check – to test his blessings, instead of live on pure faith alone. 'No,' she consoled herself. 'It is because of my faith that I can go. I will go.'

The doctor was gentle when he gave her the news, and he reached over the table to hold her hand; a gesture she looked at with numb bafflement as he explained. 'If you had come then,' he said, 'we might have been able to do something. It has spread too far now.'

A buzzing noise filled her ears as he talked, until he realised that she was not listening and grew quiet. He pulled back his hand, and after a while, he said, 'We can make it less painful.'

She looked up at him and began to laugh. She laughed so hard, and for so long, that soon it transformed into tears; hard and gut-hurting, she felt a thick hot ball of pain in her throat as she struggled to stop and find her breath.

She picked up her things and left to go home.

'I thought, death or cure,' she told her husband, alone at home. 'I'm sorry. I should have known better than to think that we could just ask.'

Farooq put his arms around her as she wept. His eyes were looking at the future.

'How long,' he asked.

'Soon,' she said. 'Three months.'

'What?' he said, suddenly awake, snapped out of the fugue into which he had slipped. 'What – there will be something to do. We can do something.'

As Fatima tried to convince him otherwise, his conviction grew. His poor wife, his dear wife, trying to keep him safe from hurt, managed everything alone. Of course these doctors would know nothing, they were locals. Poshmarg certainly did not have the best of hospitals.

'We'll go to Delhi,' he said, interrupting her litany of reasons behind why she was doomed. 'You have been to one doctor, jaan. That is not how this is done. They have simply scared you for no reason.'

Fatima stopped, confused.

'We'll go to Delhi, we'll see a specialist. There are new cures being invented every day. Three months – they cannot cure it, okay, but we will have more time. We will have so much more time.'

Fatima was soothed by the quiet confidence in his voice, the unshakeable belief in it. He did not treat her death as though it was something to fear – it was irrelevant to him because it was impossible. She clung gratefully to the idea of her own ignorance; what did she know after all, a housewife and a mother, about such complications. She had simply believed what she had been told, but of course Farooq would know better – he would know the right questions to ask, the risks to be taken, and the boundaries to be pushed.

Still, she made one last half-hearted attempt. 'It's expensive,' she said. 'What about Tufail?'

'Fatima,' he said, a finality in his voice. 'Do you think we have raised the kind of son who would want to sell his mother's life for his own comfort? He will manage. He will get that teaching job soon.' She grew silent, again uncertain. Everything had seemed so clear to her, so true. The proximity of death had felt like a filter, a magnifying glass; it had made her priorities feel so clear.

Farooq's voice was firm. 'It will be the cost of having his mother around him. That is enough.'

Days passed, and she grew weaker. Everyone seemed to know; they became more gentle with her, and talked more softly, but nobody would talk about it upfront; it was a secret that was not a secret, but one that everyone kept quiet about.

When they made their preparations to go to Delhi, only one person spoke out.

'Farooq,' Ayesha said. 'I am your sister. You know I mean this well – don't do this. I watched my father-in-law die like this. It goes by inches; stay home, keep her happy ... I should come with you, but Ahmed will be leaving so soon now.' To which Farooq almost smiled; he hugged her, said thank you, and went on his way.

When they reached Delhi, she was admitted for a flurry of tests, consultations, and appointments in a room with an air conditioner but five beds; after a week, their insurance company called them to say that it was a pre-existing condition that had not been disclosed, and so it would not be covered. He was astounded by this sleight of hand; the people on the other end of the line were relentless in their indecipherable logic. She knew before she left for her pilgrimage, didn't she? That's when they had bought her fresh insurance. Internationally applicable. But her hospital records showed her first visit to her doctor in Kashmir – there, look, in black and white, how they had noted. Glioblastoma. There was nothing left for him to say.

No matter, Farooq thought. He rang Ayesha; in two days, he had gained enough money in his account, even if he lost his family's land. It turned out that it was not enough money; not even when she was kept in the general ward, sweating silently, surrounded by people in pain, emergencies being handled dispassionately on every corner; they had one more week before he would have to give up.

It was a last-ditch attempt, the doctors said, but there had been some good results in Sweden. He thought desperately about whether he should call his friends, his relatives, to ask for help, for money, for clarity, for a decision. Finally, he sent up a prayer. 'She came to you,' he said. 'She made her pilgrimage. She is a good woman. Please.'

The test results showed an excellent outcome: against all odds, surgery could safely remove as much of the tumour as possible. He no longer had the injudicious faith as he did three months ago; but even he could not contain his joy at the taste of hope come so late. He rushed to her room, wanting to tell her the news; even if it did not work, he thought to himself – the taste of hope – he could not keep it to himself. They would share it, savour it.

'Fatima,' he said, bursting into her ward, opening her curtains. 'It's good news. I...'

Her eyes were closed, and a small smile graced her face. It was pale but not yet cold. If he tried hard enough, it could look like she was just sleeping. It had been so long since he had seen that smile, he thought to himself. She looked peaceful.

9
A Letter with No Address

In the darkness of my heart, where one settles all the unresolved phases one encounters in life, I found a letter with no address, waiting to be sent and refusing to be read. This internal battle – to allow this voice to reach out or to silence it – could reflect in the narration…

Whenever I have had the impression that I have finally let your presence out of my soul, you visit me in my dreams. Why? To keep me engaged. You've made me realise, over and over again, you don't feel the same way I felt for you when we were unruffled. I wonder: were you not involved the way you wanted me to be? As the truth finally emerged from the shadows, there was a deafening silence. From us both. It was filled with anger. Or was that just me? Did petulance and disappointment come first?

As I remember, deliberations were often slow and cumbersome, so our meetings were not particularly thrilling. And still I looked forward to them. To you. I guess you were angry that I was toying with you, and alarmed. That was the seed – or did you just want me to think so – when you decided to withdraw from how I felt for you and how you felt for me and how we felt together. Was that it? Or did you just decide, one morning, that we were never going to be one?

Was it so? – I think yes. Otherwise, how could you let me stay away from you for this long? I remember every time we fought, you would cry, trying to pull me back into your world. It was in those moments of silence that you seemed to realise your mistakes, using your tears to mend the rift between us. Those nights when you reached for me, and I told myself to stay firm, not to answer you – your calls and your texts. 'I'm dying to hear your voice again,' you said.

I knew that you would do it again. I was right, wasn't I? You would play an observer, delve into small details through which you would conclude how alienated I made you feel, would accuse me of being a sadist, finding pleasure in your longing for me. You underestimated everything. Who we were. Where we were. How much being here made us, hurt us. How our families would be. I could not let you be like that, alone in your longing. I was never so sure of myself. Admittedly, I had not felt so strongly for anyone as I did for you in those first meetings when you felt most strongly for me. I feel guilty for this intense urge, when you don't feel like that for me any more. How did it happen? At first, I did not know if these widening gaps were mostly my doing or yours. As time passed, it became clear that it was you, most of the time, who wronged me. You identified it. You took it on yourself. I – we accepted it. But how long could apologies balm the wound?

You know when I knew? That time when you showed up on my last birthday, something about your bearing – lowering your gaze so often, the lack of warmth in your kisses, your new anxieties – showed me the truth. You didn't even come to this birthday; you didn't even wish me. All my little doubts – doubting myself for doubting you – disappeared like smoke. I was both panicked and relieved.

'Hold on, I never think of my existence as separate from you; you are my pride, everything that makes my life.' Was this you in my dream tonight? Or was it the sensation of your memories? Or was it just the spirit of those times, when love would pour out of you?

Whatever. These dreams made me think again about our love, our promises to each other. Even when I know it was impossible to go back to being the way we were – living our dream. And even in the dreams, I can feel your absence in your presence. I know you would be lost to me when I open my eyes.

Your hurts always ran parallel with your love. I cannot overcome them, even if I want to. Because they have filled a corner in the space where your lack haunts me.

How could it be that you never loved me? But then, how could you surrender yourself entirely to me if you did not?

It is what is troubling me, like a dead man haunting his killer's mind. I did not kill you though, even though at some point I wanted to – not to kill you but kill your presence inside me. I worked hard for it when I felt that you had let go of your feelings for me or pretended to. Even your pretending troubled me; even as I knew you were pretending. I think you were testing me. Playing tricks. Dropping hints about another man. Peering into the depth of my love for you.

I told you then, directly. *If you're doing it to test me, you don't trust me. And if you don't trust me entirely, you'll not be faithful to me.* I told you then. I decided then that I had to leave you. I saw you banking the fire of your love. I knew I would be in the cold. Of course I was happy, very much, whenever we were together. I could see the joy and pride of being with me in your eyes, too. But we realised soon we were not well matched. I understood it and bluntly told you so.

What did you do? Instead of stopping me, you favoured your ego: I could see that you didn't want to be rejected by a person you thought was your abode for peace, your alter ego, the one you could trust and count on. But my love, this was not a game. You can't win, and you can't lose. I should have seen your self-absorption at the onset of our relationship (if it was that), which of course I had sensed, but then ignored on account of the life we were exploring together.

I knew what was troubling you: that breaking my heart would make you restless. But then first love haunts a person forever. You will always look for me in your new lovers. And I assure you, you will never find me.

I know, and you know, that this facade will come undone if and when our eyes will meet again, like the sun upon meeting the hardened snow, solidified by the cold nights.

The memories are there, the truth is there, and so is the love. It is us – we are nowhere.

10

Transience

I

Ayat was singing in her heart a lullaby of loss while watching the whirling snow. The darkness of the winter evening made the snow shine brighter against the sky, making soft drifts upon the window ledge.

Her silent song was in minor key but brushed against the memory of brighter chords – catching itself in their rhythms out of habit, only to slow down again, inevitably, into the dirge. How like the snow her life was, she thought absently to herself. Dancing in the sky, only to surrender its form and turn to tears upon the earth. She wondered whether this was the inevitable dead end of love; she considered that if all love must die, there must be a moment somewhere, the culprit with hands still stained red.

Lost in thought, Ahmed clearing his throat came as a rude intrusion in the silence that blanketed the night. The room was not so big, and she could read the upside-down words of the book he was pretending to read; he wanted her attention again, she thought. He wanted her care; he wanted her to shut the window.

Turning away from him, she looked outside, feeling the slow kindling of tension. He cleared his throat again, this time adding a sad little cough.

Her eyes flickered to the heater, looked at him, and back outside. A silent war; it was not enough for him that she was not bothering him, she thought to herself, suddenly incensed. *He must put himself first, he must see that I put him before myself. I must love him, even if he does not do the same.* He cannot take a little cold, so I can have the snow. He used to be someone who would open the window.

In that same moment, Ahmed rose.

In his mind, he had waited longingly. Expecting a touch of care. It was such a small thing, after all. He remembered the smell of her shawl, when she would sit close to him and insist upon covering them both, to keep him warm. That was Ayat. His Ayat.

He stood intently. He would keep himself warm, then, if she would not; he could close the window himself. As soon as his hand reached out, Ayat's face whipped to look at him, and the way her eyes challenged him stopped him cold.

Quietly he sat down again; now beside the electric heater, picking up his book and poring over it as though he had never left it. A moment later, the electricity went off.

Ahmed looked up from his book in pure darkness; Ayat's face limned in the silvery moonlight that reflected off the snow.

It could not be borne; he looked away and lit a candle. 'What have I done, after all,' he said to himself furiously. 'What crime have I done for her to be so cold to me.' He stood there for a minute, aching; he brought the candle down, setting it between them both, and brought himself a little closer to her under the guise of needing more light.

Ayat continued to look out the window as if he had not bothered her.

Ahmed tried again, this time more plainly: 'It seems there is no food to eat.'

Ayat was still looking out the window. The snow was peaceful. She could love it, and it would want nothing from her. She felt Ahmed's gaze upon her; she could feel the pull of it, like the faint echoes of a song whose tune is almost forgotten. If she tried to sing it again, the notes would come out wrong.

'I don't think I'd be able to sleep on an empty stomach,' Ahmed tried again. Surely, he thought, this would be enough to stress that he was hungry. Perhaps she just needed him to ask; to put down his pride, his sorrow, his waiting and just speak directly – *Ayat, will you love me still? Ayat, do I still matter? Ayat, are you still mine? Am I still yours? Ayat, please.*

There was no space left for silence; the song would need to be sung, in all its undeniable discordance.

'There is rice and dal. If you had checked, you would have seen it. If you're hungry, eat,' Ayat said quietly.

Ahmed wondered about the peace in her voice. It calmed him.

'I can't eat alone. Remember?'

'Do as you must,' Ayat said quietly, standing up and leaving him alone.

The wind was making the candle flicker. Instinctively, he reached out, and the window was closed.

II

They took wing as if they had been in a cage before they met each other.

They were caught in the sudden, swirling currents of love. Together they navigated the seasons, their days filled with everything that could not be said aloud in Poshmarg – those vast, unseen hopes that mirror the fierce, reckless dreams of the young.

One day, when the sun had turned languid, and the wind blew cold, Ahmed told Ayat he was tired; her unskilled words of love no longer conversed with his own, and he didn't see their future together. In a heartbeat, sorrow turned to rage. Where love once held the dam, it had now run dry, leaving nothing to stop the flood. Every touch had its own history when they were together; a new history now was made of endings. Anything could happen; there was no soft cushion to come home to. Everything was finished.

The pleasure of their love fled into forgetting; they pretended to be wise beyond their ages. Surely, they could be adults about this – after all, they had grown in the cold comforts of their shared homeland; what was this, compared to everything else.

But when they met in the street, a polite word extended, a little touch exchanged – of course they could have food, if there was nothing else to do. But the veneer shattered easily, each time opening the same tired wounds.

The last time that Ayat left, he was alone in the restaurant, like a lost kid in the market. Her plateful of biryani was barely touched, and her glass of water full to the brim.

Ahmed thought to himself: *I should be happy; she has set me free. I was the one who could not – would not – love her. But then, she was my friend. She could have been my friend.*

Bewilderment clashed with yearning as a song began to play, and he tried to listen more closely. 'Cholhama roshe roshe wala myani madno...'

For a moment, the ache in the lyrics reached out and claimed him.

The next day, Ayat texted him again; he saw his phone light up on his desk, and turned it over, letting it buzz until it went silent. She was probably desperate, he thought. She wanted to hear my voice, but she knew what she had done. Ahmed decided that this was a good enough reason to bid her farewell; he did it in his heart, where she did not need to see.

But fate had played its role. He was unaware that Ayat was pregnant. And he would soon loathe himself for not answering Ayat's call, where she wanted to share her news. Love was reborn, vanishing every doubt.

III

On a bright May morning, as Ahmed set out from his apartment in the city, he took a deep breath of the sun-warmed air. He felt his youth upon him, with a face upturned to the warmth; he was to teach his young students now, and after that, he would meet Ayat, he would hear her silver-quick words and her laugh; maybe she would let him hold her hand; maybe they would walk along the lake, as they did sometimes, in their little sanctuary.

He started to walk – school was only fifteen minutes away, and he thought about his students, what they would do with today's lessons. In the street, someone came running up behind him, panting; instinctively he whirled to look at him with his hands outstretched.

'It's me,' Tufail said. 'It's just me.'

'What are you doing here?' Ahmed asked, suddenly concerned. 'Why have you come down?'

'I thought I would catch you before you left,' Tufail said, still catching his breath. 'Can we go home? It will be better.'

'No,' Ahmed said, 'there's no need. Just tell me quickly what has happened. Why wait? Say it now.'

Tufail wilted before his insistent urgency.

'It's your mother,' he said, looking down at the ground. He kicked aside a stone with his toe, as Ahmed stood silently.

'She – it is that –' he tried again, and finally sighed, giving up.

He looked up at Ahmed and met his eyes. 'We did not think you should be told on the phone,' he said.

'Is she…' Ahmed asked, unable to say it out loud.

'Yes,' Tufail said. 'This morning. A car came out of nowhere when she was crossing the road. She was going to buy fruits.'

It was this detail that brought home to Ahmed the reality of this fact; his mother did indeed step out in the morning, every two or three days, to buy vegetables, fruits. The baskets in their kitchen were never empty.

'Come,' Tufail said, 'I'll take you home.'

When they sat in the car, Ahmed was silent. Tears had begun to flow, but his face was utterly still, and he did not bother to wipe them, as they dripped onto his jeans.

As they neared the house, the sound of people's sorrow met them in the street.

Death – a handy subject for anyone present there – had frisked away one man's dreams all at once. With little sunken temples and hollow cheeks, the old man reached out for Ahmed, and Ahmed was suddenly adrift; unanchored in this heaving sea of strangers.

He thought of what he could say – she was in a better place now. She was at peace now. She was with God. But Ahmed would not say the truth that he believed in, that beyond life and death, there was nothing.

Tufail slipped through the crowd of mourners, making his way to Ahmed and spoke the words written on a piece of paper so he would not have to make something anew; a solace; a note of patience; a little courage and a prayer. Ahmed, who had yet to have a moment alone, still not understanding the little feet he saw beneath the white sheet, performed the customary response: he thanked him, shook his hand, and smiled.

11

The Man from Kashmir

Evening. The theatres, art galleries, concert halls were reverberating with people rushing to their night-time delights at Covent Garden, London.

Ahmed was the first to reach, lingering outside the restaurant doors and smoking his cigarette. Rahil was the next to join, and as they crushed their smokes under their shoes, Chris came up hurriedly, his apologies filling the air.

'Is there something strange in the air today? Some spring madness?' Ahmed asked Chris, his own cheerfulness surprising him.

'It is as if the earth is flaunting itself in surprise. Everyone is out on the streets suddenly – your smiles are wider, and your people have abandoned their cardigans like chrysalises. It has made butterflies of you all. Is it you, or is it me?' He was in loose blue jeans and a faded blue striped shirt; summer's charm had met him too.

Chris chuckled. 'It's the sun, you goose. All of us Englishmen with our stiff upper lips suffer from seasonal depression, and we're finally able to remember what happiness feels like.'

'Only the English would conquer the whole world and come back home to discontent about the weather. Remember I am from Kashmir.' Ahmed laughed.

'It looks like it hit you too,' Chris said rolling his eyes. He smiled gently, and Ahmed looked away. 'It's good to see our old friend back. You look happy.'

Rahil clicked his teeth at this show of sentimentalism, knowing it would send Ahmed scurrying back into shyness. 'Yes, yes, don't relapse again. Come now, it's a good day. Any good news?'

'No. Nothing yet,' Ahmed answered with a sigh.

'That's rough, man,' Chris said. Ahmed glanced at him with disbelief for a moment but quickly recovered.

'Yes. Today marks a hundred days.' He looked away. 'How long has it been since you knew whether your family was alive, Chris?'

'Oh – Ahmed, man, I didn't mean...'

'It's fine. I'm sorry. I snapped. I shouldn't have.'

Ahmed's eyes were wet, and he looked away.

They would not understand him, he realised again. He was with them, but he was not with them.

Cool hands suddenly covered his eyes, and a familiar scent wafted in the air.

'Guess who?'

He smiled. 'The most beautiful girl in the world.'

Harriet laughed and pulled up a chair. Ahmed realised she had never met his friends before and made quick work of introductions. As the conversation started to flow effortlessly, he joined in when asked direct questions.

'Ahmed – come back,' Harriet said, tugging his sleeve fondly.

'What?' he said. 'Sorry, I missed that.'

'You'll come for the sit-in, won't you?'

'What sit-in?'

'The one for Kashmir. They're calling for Article 370 to be reinstated, and against the communication shutdown.'

Ahmed looked slightly dazed. He scanned his surroundings – soft voices of the people around, their smiling faces, the clink of their glasses full of what looked like liquid gold. 'Yes,' he said. 'Sit-in. For Kashmir. Of course I'll be there.'

It was getting late, and they promised to meet the following weekend. Ahmed's eyes kept flickering between Chris, Rahil, and Harriet as if it were the last time he was seeing them.

We live at the mercy of the seasons' whims, never certain of the hour ahead. But perhaps that is Nature's trick: it keeps us so engrossed in the struggle of the 'now' that we lose our sense of wonder. The great mystery of life becomes a cheap distraction, something we no longer have the space or the breath to truly contemplate.

In Ahmed's diary that night a single couplet found home.

...with this endless night the soft voices curved as thunder,

The missing, the dead, the living – evaporated all at once.

***

Harriet was in her bedroom. She had not been able to stop staring at the wall blank eyed. Her mother had forced her to talk about it.

'I loved him, Mummy. Still do. Love him. Like nothing I've ever loved before. I felt like I could live off that love and want nothing in return. It made more space for itself, it was so... Nothing else mattered.'

She breathed slowly, deliberately.

'I never told him, but I thought he knew. We… You know how it is – early days. I was worried he wouldn't love me as more than a friend, you know, because he loved his friends, he loved us all. It was keeping me up at nights – I would find myself wondering how I would tell him. I had to tell him. I kept going in circles, and I wanted to turn it off, you know. That's when I saw his email. I saw his email, and I thought he has heard me. He was thinking of me too. I won't have to ask; he will tell me.'

She was quiet, her head bowed, her small hand clutching her mother's.

'The beginning of that email – I couldn't understand it – I can't stop thinking about it. If I could have done something had I understood it. He said, "I was looking for someone who could understand me, who knows the quiet ache of becoming a ghost in one's own living city … the state where all else – achievement, struggles, everything concerning existence counts for nothing." I couldn't understand it, what he was saying, but it felt important. I wanted to understand him. I wanted to reply with something perfect, something that could make him realise I understood him, that … well.

I don't know how I thought I was going to do that. He was talking about dying.'

'Harriet,' her mum said softly. 'You couldn't have known.'

She looked up.

'He sent it to all of us, Ma, and none of us knew. None of us realised. I was busy thinking about what I could respond with that would make him love me.'

Her eyes were focused again on the wall, and her mother sighed.

For a moment, he returned to her – or the ghost of him did – not the riddle of his politics or the theoretical framework of his grief, but the man as he was. She remembered the specific, grounding weight of him: the way the light caught the rough texture of his sweater, the scent of cold air and tobacco that clung to his skin, and the rhythmic tap of his fingers against a table when he was deep in thought. Those were the things she could recognise, the parts of him she could hold in her gaze.

But his heart? His mind? Those were vast, shadowed territories she had only ever glimpsed through a glass, darkly. She had spent so much time trying to decode the man, she had forgotten to simply be with him while he was still solid.

'I knew the shape of his hands,' she whispered, her voice fracturing. 'But I never knew who he truly was.'

'Come on now,' her mother said. 'It's going to be all right.'

***

'See, I knew Ahmed, and I knew Harriet was in love with him – it was obvious, right, all over her face. And he was … he wasn't cold, exactly, but his diary was full of love poetry, and it was all for Ayat, his wife.' Rahil was talking to his friend at the restaurant he owned.

Peter nodded, cleaning the glasses at the bar while they talked.

'Does she know?' he asked Rahil.

'No,' he said. 'At least… Look, Peter, I don't know what the university is doing, right? But I tried to get in touch with his family. His wife, his uncle. I could call the embassy and ask, but that means someone in uniform will go up to their house, and right now that could mean trouble for them.'

He laughed joylessly. 'The last thing I want to do is get his wife killed by trying to get them the news that her husband has killed himself.'

Peter froze briefly, seeming to digest this information.

'It's that bad?' he asked tentatively.

Rahil raised his head and looked at him. 'Yes,' he said. 'It's that bad.'

He looked away. 'It's not like I can even blame you. I don't think even I could really understand what was going on. I can't visit Kashmir, you know. I've lived here for decades, but there, I'd be a Pakistani first.'

Peter looked troubled. 'It doesn't seem right, does it, the times we're living in, we can't tell them that Ahmed died.'

Rahil laughed under his breath. 'I think I understand him a little better now, you know. He told me once that if he dies here, his family would never forgive him, because his death would become a mystery to them.'

'Tell me more about him,' Peter said. 'There's another thing I don't understand. He got out, didn't he? It's bad there now, you're saying, but he was here, wasn't he. It was good for him.'

Rahil considered this.

'I met him when Chris brought him to my restaurant, actually. He said a professor from your country needed help understanding his dreams.'

'I forgot about that.' Peter smiled. 'You and the dreams.'

Rahil said, 'My friend, you are not like many Englishmen, but you betray yourself here. My father was a dream interpreter before me, and I might have degrees in psychology now, but I'm still proud to be called a dream interpreter just like he was.'

'What was he dreaming then?'

'I suppose it can't hurt to tell you now,' Rahil mused. 'It was even before the reading down of Article 370 – do you know what that is?'

'Something like – no, actually. It reminded me of the Troubles?'

'Good enough,' Rahil said. 'Something like a fight for home, against people who want to take it from you and make it theirs, I suppose. But yes. Chris introduced us, at which point he also realised that Kashmir and Pakistan are not, in fact, the same country.'

'White people,' Peter said dryly. 'We're all the same. Tell the dreams though!'

'Sure. Let me read you a page from his diary, which he wrote once after having a bad dream.'

'Hold on. Can I see it for myself?' Rahil paused and then pushed the book towards him. Who was there now to take offence?

Looking at the first pages, Peter said, 'Not winning any prizes for his handwriting, is he? It looks like he was taking notes in class, a college boy in a hurry.'

'That may be, but Peter, read the words. Here, look at this bit. "My logic is simple: don't explain yourself to those who presume they know all that's in your head and are unremittingly looking for your slip-ups; instead, force them to confront their own mindlessness."'

'Unthinking,' Peter said.

'Perhaps he was,' Rahil said. 'He was living alone, for the first time in his life, in such a diverse atmosphere, here in London. He had trained himself to live an independent life. It's what he had wanted since he was a child, and then after he got in the master's course at King's, he could finally move here.'

They were quiet.

'He wanted to bring his family here and settle down. He was well known back home, but here, he was just – no, that's not it. He didn't care about being known. He was well loved. He had a job, one he enjoyed doing; he worked hard for it and it suited him.'

'What did he do?' Peter asked.

'What does any brown man with a degree in the humanities do in academia?' Rahil said.

'Colonial studies. Postcolonial literature of India and Africa. He had also been working on a book about Kashmir – specifically, the application of postcolonial theory to the region. He maintained that postcolonial theory was insufficient to articulate the complex political landscape of Kashmir, because Kashmir's ongoing status meant it was still being colonised by nations that were themselves once colonised. He would often discuss with me how the British colonial residue was being leveraged by previously colonised nations. He aimed to provide a theoretically grounded framework to the nuances of the Kashmir issue, yielding a localised solution. He also wanted to teach the Modernists. Joyce, Yeats, Eliot – he loved them.

'I know that one,' Peter said. 'Indeed there will be time / To wonder / "Do I dare?" and "Do I dare?" / Time to turn back and descend the stair…'

The unexpected note from the stolid man made Rahil look at him in surprise. 'A levels,' he said dismissively. 'The dreams man, tell me his dreams!'

'Right, yes. See, I never knew that an academic would have liked an interpretation from a man like me. See – I am not an academic at all. And I had always been drawn to deep thinkers.

When Chris told me about him, I was thrilled. Not because he would know me as a dream interpreter, which I always loved, but because we came from similar, if not the same, worlds. Despite all odds, we would have something in common, I thought. When he came, he was this neat man in his neat suit, tallish, with a little beard. He had a dimple, you know, though it was only visible rarely. He was as handsome as they say – no, Peter, back home, we grow up hearing of the beauty of Kashmiri people, and well, it was true.'

He sighed. 'The first thing I said to him was in Urdu. Pardes me apni zubaan mein baatein karne mein apna hi maza hai.'

'What?' Peter asked.

'It is a rare pleasure to speak in your mother tongue in a foreign land.'

'Ah, I hear you. Did he speak your language? You said it wasn't the same country?'

'Oh yes, he did. It's not the same country but we shared the same language – India does too. Anyway. We talked about that, about our homes. He was friendly, but he wasn't so easy to understand.'

'And then he told you about his dreams?'

'Yes. Horrible stuff. Ahmed walking through an orchard where the trees aren't made of wood, but of rusted iron and ticking gears. Instead of fruit, the branches hang with heavy, glass-blown lungs that turn black as he touches them. In another dream, he is sitting at a dinner table with his family. Everyone is laughing, but they are eating handfuls of dry salt. He looks down and notices the floor is dissolving into deep, black water. He tries to scream, but when he opens his mouth, a small silver bird flies out and strikes the window, which turns into a mirror. Then the vision changes: Ahmed is trying to fold a massive paper map of his neighbourhood, but the more he folds it, the larger it gets. The ink on the map starts to liquefy and run off the page, staining his hands permanent indigo. Suddenly, the "house" on the map begins to grow teeth and starts chewing the paper he is standing on.'

'Were they related to his memories?'

'No, I don't think so. They weren't just like… It's different. He had seen his decapitated head in many of his dreams. In another dream, his wife dialled a rotary phone carved from bone. In his London flat, the receiver didn't ring – it exhaled a thick, white fog. His cleaner calmly vacuumed the mist into a canvas bag, tied it shut, and fed the bag into the mouthpiece. On the other end, his wife dropped the phone; it shattered into a pomegranate that spilled stones instead of seeds.'

'What did you get from his dreams?'

'I refused to answer him straightaway. He gave me his book of poetry before leaving, and later I found he had left his diary. I didn't peek, but when I met him and tried to return it, he said that he had left it so I would read it. I was surprised, and I couldn't wait to go through it now that I had his permission.

'While thinking about him, I recall an eerie dream a person had shared with me last year. That person had seen a couple screaming about the noise of a crowded world. Their solution was a strange, frantic ritual – plugging each other's ears to drown out the masses, choosing to hear only the echo of their own voices in the hollow of their skulls.'

'I don't understand.'

'There was a haunting geometry to Ahmed's dreams. I saw them as a death-knell, or perhaps a confession of his fractured love for Kashmir. I needed one more conversation, one more look at the man behind the visions, and I did. But…'

Peter silently placed a hand on Rahil's. It wasn't just a gesture of comfort; it was an acknowledgement that their friend was now a ghost they both had to carry.

'… the diary spoke louder than he ever could.'

12
Into the Void

Ayat craved to see the youthful gaze of Aydin once again before she was awake.

Decades had passed in war. The world watched and pleaded, yet the devastation did not recede. India and Pakistan held their ground, and Kashmir paid the price in blood and soil.

Both countries wanted sole ownership, which screamed doomsday for the residents of Poshmarg, as it did for the rest of Kashmir. Nearly a third of the population of Poshmarg had been wiped out, mostly killed by bombs and airstrikes. In the ensuing chaos of the threat of nuclear bombs, protective isolation became the only resort.

It was against the backdrop of this chaos that it was made clear to the people of Poshmarg that their only hope of survival were the bunkers. They dug until the thunder of the bombs grew faint and the surface grew distant – tombs turned into homes. These were depths one couldn't easily climb out of, carved wide enough to hold the ghost of the world they had lost.

When the bombs fell on Poshmarg, they left a thick crust of heavy metal that melted into the earth.

Safe underground, Ayat felt, more warmly, that there was still a possibility for life – to continue how they used to live in the old times, before this war. When she had still been young and Poshmarg was the most beautiful place in the world.

This new reality, its harsh environment, made her understand more of her nature and of those who surrounded her. Humanity's dark side seemed impossible to suppress; the more it was denied, the more violently it resurfaced, as if seeking retribution for being ignored. So she thought, it was best to pull oneself together, accept the challenges and move on.

Despite knowing she could never go home again, she hoped to. She knew if Aydin ever returned, the stark truth of their displacement would drain the joy from his arrival. She thought of herself as a robot – every day the same set of movements, the same outcomes. But she remembered being more than a machine

– her emotions, dreams, and nostalgia separated her from one. But how would Aydin's travelling back to their normal home be possible? She was conscious of surveillance satellites wheeling through Poshmarg. This urge to escape from her very refuge kept her from fully embracing her new reality; she was always only half present, her mind pulled away by a constant, gnawing anxiety for Aydin.

Ayat had not stopped Aydin from moving out of Poshmarg. She made Aydin believe in himself, work hard and achieve his dreams of studying abroad, like his father. It was very difficult for the both of them to live without each other, but they were strong enough to sacrifice their comforts for the sake of the other. She let Aydin explore the world.

They were witnessing a brutal war, even when the potential of the war going nuclear was a possibility, but one taken lightly.

Overnight, the city saw a vertiginous rise in temperature, almost melting the veneer of their iron compartments. Ayat felt it as soon as she woke up in the middle of the night and found herself drenched in sweat. The strident siren called for her to stay indoors, where conditions were favourable enough to survive. She knew the others would also be sheltering as she was

– there was no need to go out for the community prayer today. As she settled into her bunk, she weighed the stillness of her dreams against the forlorn happy world that she had lost. She remembered the early days.

Scary as it was, she had learned to explore this new way of living in this strange new world. Her faith, which had led her to this new life as an imam, beneath Poshmarg, had been steadily eroding.

Was it because she was weary of performing the same religious rituals again and again, until they had lost all meaning? Or was it because she had explored the unknown – a world larger than what her religion had imagined?

Her faith was holding on to her like a loose button stuck to a shirt by a single flimsy thread.

She was well aware of it. And she wanted to bind it again, sturdily before it fell and was lost, to keep it fixed there, forever, like she had done many times before. But she found herself wondering – was there any faith which could hold itself firmly when accompanied by doubt?

Even if her suspicions were weak, compared to her belief, she felt as though the human self could only keep one thing: doubt or faith. Both faith and uncertainty couldn't – wouldn't – exist together. Even if they did, and she knew that many had gone through this valley of darkness to emerge into the light, with their faith intact, it still disrupted her routine every day.

Doubt unsettled her as quickly as faith held her together.

She found herself inhabiting the strange space where doubt itself became an article of faith, looming large over her. But she found herself cringing away from the finality of full acceptance. She still wanted to fight for her dream – to go back to the place where her faith lived, where even the air was pure and free from all this noise. But these were private storms, locked deep inside. She wasn't yet ready to give them voice.

She wondered exactly when she had lost her faith. Was it her pessimism and detachment first? Had that lit the spark of doubt? When had this spark engulfed the entire sanctuary of her faith? What was left of it – the ashes – and where could she still find her complete trust in God?

Ayat had not wilfully begun her relationship to her community as an imam – it had taken place unexpectedly. When she arrived, she had joined the group of Muslims living underground, who began to serve the faith to survive the violence outside.

This group had a list of tasks to deliver in this suffocating new reality. One among them was to build the Jamia Masjid for all the Muslims of Poshmarg, which they did. It was a makeshift masjid, a skeletal version of the mosques they had left behind. With no minarets to call the dawn or domes to catch the light, it was defined only by its bare walls and the simple mihrab etched into the bunker's grey stone.

But not even the pressures of living the bunker life could hold back their essential humanity. The group could not help but split into factions as soon as they began to practise their faith properly.

Some members rebelled against Ayat, a woman, being their imam; some fought against the rule that daily prayer should be five times a day, advocating for it to be performed only once or twice, given they no longer saw the sunrise or sunset; some of them thought of reducing the number of fasting days as well, given the poor supply of rations throughout the year.

Ayat had always had an ardent belief that the practice of faith needed a careful balance between a devotee's discipline, and the natural rhythm of what she was called to do. She could not believe that a new world would demand old sacraments.

'Ayat,' someone said out loud, urgently, banging at her door. The news broke out that the uniformed men had attacked.

Ayat got up and opened the door. 'What is it? What has happened? Why aren't you in your bunker?'

'It was perhaps missiles, not nuclear. You see – they've – they've hit us this time.'

Ayat was perplexed. 'Yes, I thought it might be. The heat, you know. But why are you here?'

'Ayat, they hit the masjid. They won't let us in, but I thought … you know… Please,' the man said. 'The whole place is burned up. We could not – we could only find Aydin's hand.'

Silently, amid the still shrieking sirens, he leaned forward and put a single ring – the ring that Ayat had given Aydin just before he left home some eighteen months ago – in her hand.

'What?' Ayat said. 'What are you saying? Where is Aydin?'

'I have to go,' the man said wretchedly. 'All I know is that Aydin had returned. He was out in Poshmarg looking for you when he was recognised by our men and brought back under cover of night. Once he heard you were the imam, he must have asked for the masjid. I imagine he wanted to surprise you there.' Ayat noticed through her shock that her face was covered in soot, sweat and tears forming wet pathways through it.

While the people spoke of angels falling from grace, Ayat was shaken by the tragedy. She saw herself as a failed Daedalus, a mother who had crafted wings that could not withstand the heat, watching helplessly as her son burned.

The haunting, which her son's death invited, assembled in the corners of both Ayat's reason and emotion. She went silently through each day, drowning in her guilt.

Her faith, already teetering on the edge of dissolution, boiled into a fury of unanswerable questions. Why her, she thought, incensed – she who had lived her life devoted to her faith.

Was it punishment for her doubt? The questions that had kept her up as a teenager, which had been obliterated in her study of the faith, now rose again. Doubt made a void in her, taking the place that held her love for Ahmed and Aydin. The thoughts chased their tails inside her head – did she lose her faith because she lost her son? Or did she lose her son because she had lost her faith?

She forced herself into thinking the existential questions that used to disturb her. Why would it happen to her, she thought, when she had lived all her life according to the divine plan?

Now, after devoting her entire life to this faith, she wondered how again she was feeling as she did in those days when she was trying to survive the death of her husband: when the doubt had created a void in her. And she turned restless. Ironically, she reviewed all her life as futile – something believers took positively and used the belief for their own good. It was different for Ayat.

She felt as though she had found an answer to a question she had had for long: why did piety follow tragedy?

She thought of how the most ardent believers had their faith tested with great grief. Whenever she had countered these kinds of thoughts before, her belief had saved her: an extraordinary eternal life awaited the pious after this life. But now, she couldn't stop excavating the value of her life. The more she thought, the guiltier she felt. Had she lost it all? She thought, what if this was her only life and what if there was no afterlife, no heaven, no God, and now no Ahmed, no Aydin.

She viewed the quintessential things of her life, how different it all could have been if she were without any faith. The kind of life she was so proud of suddenly turned against her. Simple living, which she considered bliss, was now a trap.

The greatest tragedy for her was that she could not reveal her rebellious inner self to the world, even to her closest companions. She feared she would lose them too. What would happen if the people discovered her sudden disbelief? Would they kill her? Or would they silently remove her as their imam? And what would her life be then? Would she even have one – and would she still be alien, alone in the world, as she was now? She numbly went to pray.

As the speakers expounded on the belief in the one, she understood dispassionately that her thoughts were blasphemy. She knew well that this blasphemy could lead her to hell. That had not worried her before.

But suddenly, she recalled her family, and she was flooded with guilt: in the inferno she wouldn't be able to see her family. Ahmed, Aydin; their uncomplicated faith would lead them to heaven. Tears trickled through the wrinkled strands threaded on her face; the people watching thought she was yet again thinking of her son. She left silently. At her abode, she dropped to her knees in prostration and begged God to forgive her.

She would never give doubt room again.

In her sleep, Ayat dreamed about her return to life…

She had just returned from the clinic when she told her husband Ahmed about their pregnancy. They tasted happiness as never before. They were delighted that they would finally have someone in their life who would give a new shine to their place in the world, who would make everything they owned more precious. They renovated their house, requested Ayesha, Farooq and Tufail to stay with them in London, to which they happily agreed.

Their joy was contagious – it was a dream coming true: their desire to have a happy family. Ahmed redesigned his study as well; he wanted to have shelves of children's literature, which would cause his child to seek out his father's company. Those were the most beautiful and most exciting days for them. And finally, when Aydin was born, it seemed to them that God had given them everything. Though both Ayat and Ahmed saw themselves in their son, she was also in awe of how unique he was – his deep cleverness and a natural ease that felt like the cure for what Ayat herself never found.

Ahmed and Ayat made sure that their son had every privilege she did not – especially, the best of education. Aydin never stopped making them proud, and the parents were both overjoyed at his every success. Ahmed and Ayat were living the unimaginably perfect life. She opened her eyes, and the sweet sunshine of the dream gave way to the iron box. For a minute, she was safe from the ravages of the truth: her husband and son were still dead. Her family was still lost to her. The sweetness of her dream nearly broke her in this comparison, and she wept into her hands. The only thing now was death – the only way to ever see them again.

But she could not.

No Muslim who took their own life would see the gates of heaven.

She knew then that she had died long ago – she merely had to wait now.

With these thoughts, she was able to sleep again. In her sleep, she searched restlessly for the thread that would bring her back to her beloveds, and finally, she saw them. Her husband and her beautiful son. They were in a garden, happy and playing with stars in their hands, and they were waiting for her to join them.

Epilogue

Shikwa

Kashmir is breaking up with me.
We had our highs and lows,
But we also had love, didn't we?
True love?
It must have been. It must have been.

We dreamed of making a little paradise,
Worked tirelessly on it.
Our little home, our safe nest,
Our blood, sweat and tears,
Our days and our nights.
We had it, didn't we?
Almost within our reach?
It must have been. It must have been.

Kashmir is breaking up with me.
She's leaving me now.
I can't... She won't... She is...
I can't believe she's capable of such cruelty!

Epilogue

Let us now take a tally.
The truth and the lies.
The truth and the truth.
What you said to me, what I confessed to you.

You said I was special,
I almost believed it.
Not that I'm Ashraful Makhluqaat,
Because I was born out of you,
For you.

You were the jewel, a crown.
You were in my hands,
Kings lay their eyes on you,
Coveting, wanting. Always.
Who could blame them?
Ashoka, Kushan,
Mughal, Dogra,
India, Pakistan.
But you were mine.
Your heart was mine.

Now they say I can't take care of you,
You can't survive alone.
You would be too tempting,
Helen immortal,
Who would not go to war for you?
Who did your heart belong to?

Epilogue

When Paris stole you away.
Did you not run, soft-footed, your hand in mine,
I fought for you, and
You fought for me too.
I was you, and you were me,
Who can take you, O part of me?
Where could you go, where I would not follow?

My freedom was sold for your weight in gold,
I cried, I rattled the bars of my cage,
I raised my hand to my jailor's face,
And rubbed away his tears,
Beaten black and blue until I identified,
That brown is the new white.

I did not cease,
I could not fight,
My arms behind my back.
But still. A moment came!
The jailor's smile, as clear as morning dawn,
And the door was about to open.

It was going to open, wasn't it?
It must have been. It must have been.
Another face now, another time.
When I am sold now, I do not know,
How much I cost.
It is just for now,

Epilogue

My new jailor croons.
For my own good.
How long have I been here, waiting?
What do I know of the world outside?

Where were you in all this?
Did you watch?
I am at war with myself and you,
How could you abandon me?
How could I save you now,
Who left first?

It was so easy now for them.
I didn't have you.
She let us in, they whispered in the night.
She's left you, and she knows.

And the worst: I saw you dining with them.
And then sleeping with them.
You said it was all to help.
Did you do this to me?

How could you do this to me!
You let them on your body.
And I was made an unwanted guest in my own house.
They stole my rights, broke my home,

Epilogue

Starved me, whipped me,
Left me bleeding.
They took my bread and liberation from me.

And you witnessed all of this in silence.
Why are you so quiet?
Why won't you say anything?
Will you be polite? Should I speak
In a softer tone.
Am I scaring you, my darling,
My love? My love, this was all for you.

You needed the comfort,
I know that. I understand.

You've overthrown many monarchies,
Survived so many wars,
You carry those deep scars, yes.
Exposed on your body, laying them on me and
your history.

You needed the relief,
From your children, clamouring always,
Seeking out your hands,
From the urge to shake them, hard, once,
twice,
Until they are quiet.

Epilogue

And now you blame me for all this anarchy.
You say there's no freedom without sacrifice.
Whose freedom? Whose sacrifice?

The children are quiet, my love,
Look what you have done,
Look at their little bodies on the floor…

Do you want them back?
Do you want me back?

I am lost, and I don't know my way back home.
I'm walking back to you, my love,
My footprints now bloody.

I'll always come back, my jaan,
My one true love.

See – you asked, and I'm walking.
The glass is pressing deeper now.
You want this?

I love you.
I loved you.
I love you.
It hurts, my love.
Why do you want to hurt me?

Epilogue

Why are you saying this,
Stop it – I'm yours, you said so.
I'm blessed, you said so.
My life. My beating heart. My curse.
Have I been a fool for you?

You told the uniformed men that I am violent,
Vicious and trying to kill you.

I don't know what hurts worse,
The gun is digging into my chest now,
But I am looking at your eyes.

My love,
Come now,
Is this my last moment?
Will you not look at me with tenderness?
You're breaking my heart.

Come now, we'll go home,
I'll hold your hand, we'll lie down,
Under the chinar, and watch the sky,
Through the leaves,
Kashmir, sweetheart, please stop.

Stop now, come on,
I don't want to die young.

Epilogue

Tell them, do not shoot.
They'll listen to you.
Please stop them.
Please!
Stop!

Acknowledgements

Alhamdulilah!

I owe the person I have become to my parents, Mohammad Ramzan and Ayesha, and to my brothers, Musaddiq, Shoib, and Najmus Saqib. Alongside being my life's companion, you have all been my foundation and my light – shaping my soul with your love and guiding my hand with your strength. I also offer my sincere thanks to my uncles, cousins, and extended family for their unwavering support and encouragement.

To Manzoor Ahmad, my uncle and teacher, who thoughtfully helped me choose English literature as the subject for my college studies.

To Bouba, my late grandmother, whose simplicity remains our guiding light.

To Bubb, my late maternal grandfather, who lived through his stories.

I am also profoundly grateful to my teachers, who helped me rediscover hope in literature and find a path forward.

I am especially grateful to Aamer Hussein for discovering the writer in me and offering the vital encouragement needed to begin my literary journey. I am also thankful to Amit Chaudhuri for his suggestions and to Tabish Khair for his support.

To my friends, both old and new: thank you for the generosity of your time, your patience with my queries, and your continued friendship. I am particularly moved by, and grateful to, the friends who so courageously entrusted me with the truths of their lives in Kashmir.

The early drafts of several chapters appeared in *Critical Muslim*, *Himal Southasian*, *The Bombay Review*, *Outlook*, *The Aleph Review*, *Khabar*, and Kitaab, among others. I appreciate the editors and publishers of these journals and magazines for their early encouragement. The book has evolved significantly.

I am also thankful to A Suitable Agency and Bloomsbury India for their interest in this manuscript, especially Naomi Barton, Chirag Thakkar, and Chakrika Pandey for their keen observations and impeccable edits in shaping this novella, and also to Ambar Sahil Chatterjee for his guidance.